THE
DRAGOMAN'S
STORY

A Selection of Recent Titles by Michael Pearce

THE MAMUR ZAPT AND THE DONKEY-VOUS

THE MAMUR ZAPT AND THE MEN BEHIND

THE MAMUR ZAPT AND THE SPOILS OF EGYPT

THE MAMUR ZAPT AND THE RETURN OF THE CARPET

THE MAMUR AND THE GIRL IN THE NILE

DMITRI AND THE ONE-LEGGED LADY

DMITRI AND THE MILK DRINKERS

DEATH OF AN EFFENDI

THE DRAGOMAN'S STORY

Michael Pearce

This first world edition published in Great Britain 2000 by
SEVERN HOUSE PUBLISHERS LTD of
9–15 High Street, Sutton, Surrey SM1 1DF.
This first world edition published in the USA 2000 by
SEVERN HOUSE PUBLISHERS INC of
595 Madison Avenue, New York, N.Y. 10022.

British Library Cataloguing in Publication Data

Pearce, Michael, 1933 July 23-
    The dragoman's story
    1. Nightingale, Florence, 1820-1910 - Journeys - Nile River - Fiction
    2. Flaubert, Gustave, 1821-1880 - Journeys - Nile River - Fiction
    3. Egypt - Description and travel - Fiction
    I. Title
    823.9'14 [F]

    ISBN 0-7278-5569-7

Typeset by Palimpsest Book Production Ltd.,
Polmont, Stirlingshire, Scotland.
Printed and bound in Great Britain by
MPG Books Ltd, Bodmin, Cornwall.

Acknowledgements

In this book I have drawn on numerous works by Victorian travellers, but acknowledge a particular debt to *Letters from Egypt* by Florence Nightingale, selected and introduced by Anthony Sattin (Barrie and Jenkins, London, 1987) and *Flaubert in Egypt*, translated and edited by Frances Steegmuller (Bodley Head, 1972).

One wonders that people come back from Egypt and
live lives as they did before.

Florence Nightingale

One

Curiously, they never met, unless you count that sighting at Bulaq the first day. And that was hardly auspicious.

"An English family? Hideous! The mother looked like a sick old parrot."

"Oh, come!" I said.

"That eyeshade! Like a beak."

"That was *not* her mother. There *was* no mother. Mrs Bracebridge is merely a friend."

"Why make a friend out of a parrot?"

"The English are animal lovers," said Maxime.

I could not persuade them. They refused to join forces, and so there I was with two parties in town at the same time.

It had been bad enough at Bulaq. I had naturally expected both parties to be on the passenger steamer and had taken up my position accordingly. What had been my consternation when, glancing along the quay to where the baggage steamer had just tied up, I saw descending the gangway what could only be the French party I was expecting! Happily, the Bracebridge party, which I had already spotted high up on the top deck, was showing no inclination to join the mêlée pushing and jostling to disembark so I was able to dart along the quay and catch the Frenchmen just as they set foot on shore.

"Welcome to Cairo!" I cried, seizing each of them by the arm and waving away the importuning porters and drivers. "Your transport awaits you!"

I forced a way through the crowd to where Selim had the donkeys ready. I sometimes find that people are a little put off when they see the donkeys. The Frenchmen did indeed waver but then embraced the exotic enthusiastically, pausing only to murmur something about their baggage.

"Already in hand, messieurs! It will follow by camel."

Maxime leaped upon one of the donkeys, his long legs dangling down almost to the ground.

"A race!" he cried. "A race!"

Then they were off, Selim running ahead of them cracking his whip to clear a passage, with the two Frenchmen bouncing up and down on their donkeys as they set off along the grand allée leading to the city.

I hurried back to the passenger steamer. The Bracebridges were now standing on the quay, a little, defensive, European island beset by a sea of importunate Eastern humanity which pressed in upon it at all points. The male of the party was attempting to ward them off, and growing fierce.

I pushed my way through the crowd towards him.

"Mr Bracebridge?"

He turned, surprised.

"Sir?"

"Thomas Wood." I bowed. "At your service, sir. Mr Murray, our consul here, asked me to come in case I could be of some assistance."

Bracebridge looked round at the throng of porters, donkey drivers, dragomans and beggars.

"Well, yes," he said, "I think you could."

I led the ladies to the barouche and put them under the protection of the driver and his outrunner. Then I went with Mr Bracebridge to fetch the baggage.

"There's hardly going to be room," said Mr Bracebridge doubtfully, eyeing the barouche.

"Oh, the baggage will travel separately."

I picked four likely drivers and they began to load the cases on to their camels.

"How extraordinary!" said one of the ladies, a tall, thin, dark girl.

"Not at all, madame," I said, climbing in beside her. "Almost everything is transported by camel here."

"Not donkey?"

"We use donkeys for riding. It's by far the best way to get around."

"I don't think—" began the girl.

"We used donkeys in Greece," said Mrs Bracebridge. "It's quite easy when you know how."

"It is, I suppose, the way Our Lord travelled," observed the tall girl gravely.

After which, conversation, not surprisingly, languished.

English parties, I have found, tend to be either biblical or military. The military ones are on their way to India, breaking their journey for a few days in the more comfortable surroundings of Cairo before proceeding to Suez to catch a steamer for the last part of their journey. The biblical ones come to see the newly excavated ruins. They spend longer in the country, which is preferable for me on financial grounds but, increasingly these days, they, too, merely break their journey at Cairo. The ruins are upstream at places like Luxor and Kom Ombo and Assuan and to get to them you have to go by boat.

"Is it your intention to proceed up river?" I asked Mr Bracebridge.

"Indeed, it is. We hope to spend about a fortnight here and then carry on to Ipsamboul and Philae."

"For that you will need to hire a boat."

"So I understand."

"May I venture to advise you, sir? Do take care! Not every *dahabeeyah* – the kind of boat you will be needing – that you will be shown will be entirely suitable."

Mr Bracebridge looked thoughtful.

"If I can be of any assistance . . ."

"I would be greatly obliged."

"Not at all!"

Not at all. The commission would have to be shared but would still be enough to see me through the summer. I sat back pleased. There might even be a chance of a second commission if the French party turned up trumps. I would speak to them that evening when I went round to settle them into their hotel.

The parties were staying at different hotels, the Bracebridges at the Hôtel de l'Europe, the Frenchmen at the Hôtel d'Orient. I had regretted this initially, since I had hoped to bring the two parties together and run them as one. It was already becoming apparent, however, that they differed considerably in character and I soon realised that it would never have done. In any case, the Bracebridges moved on after a fortnight, and during that fortnight the parties pursued quite separate paths. So it was that they never, in fact, actually met.

Afterwards, when they had both become famous, I rather regretted that I never succeeded in bringing Florence Nightingale and Gustave Flaubert together.

"But, surely, Mr Wood, if I wear a veil and ugly, as you have prescribed, I have made sufficient concession to Muslim susceptibility."

I had become sufficiently acquainted by now with ladies' garments to know that an ugly was a sort of shade worn as an appendage to the bonnet.

"The ugly, Miss Nightingale, is merely for protection

5

against the glare. The veil, it is true, is a concession to Muslim susceptibility, but I am afraid it will not be enough if you wish to go into a mosque."

"Mr Wood is quite right, my dear," said Mrs Murray. We had gone out into the garden of the consulate to see the hippopotamus. It was five months old and a new acquisition. "It would be out of the question to go as you are."

"It is really out of the question for a woman anyway," said her husband.

"To go to a mosque? But surely she may go to worship?" asked Miss Nightingale.

"We-ell . . . up to a point."

"I don't understand."

Mrs Murray intervened. "In this country, Miss Nightingale, as I am sure you know, women seldom appear in public. That applies to the mosque too. There is usually a special gallery, screened off, where they attend on feast days, the older women, that is, but—"

"And otherwise they are excluded?"

"Women do go," said Mr Murray, "but not usually at a time of public worship."

Miss Nightingale was silent.

"I am sure it would be all right," said Mrs Murray, "if you were appropriately dressed."

"And went at a suitable time," I said.

"I should very much like to go," said Miss Nightingale.

6

Mr Murray remained unhappy, but faced with the opposition of two such formidable ladies was obliged to acquiesce. His wife produced the clothes and Miss Nightingale retired with Mrs Bracebridge to put them on: first, an immense blue silk sheet with a hole in the middle to put your head through, Mrs Bracebridge recounted later; then a white strip of muslin to go over the nose ("like a horse's nosebag," explained Miss Nightingale), which was fastened by a stiff band passing between the eyes and then going back over and behind the head ("halter," said Miss Nightingale); then a white veil; and, finally, "a black silk balloon" which was pinned, apparently, to the top of the head and had two loops, one at each end, through which one put one's wrists.

Thus attired, the ladies paraded before us. We pronounced them charming. Muffled voices gasped that charm was purchased at the price of respiration and that the sooner we set out the better.

It had been agreed that while we men would be close at hand we would not actually enter the mosque, since that would give the game away. Instead, the ladies were accompanied by Mr Murray's janissary, divested of his uniform for the occasion. At the last moment, however, Mr Murray suggested that I should slip in by one of the other entrances and watch from behind the pillars in case help should be required.

I saw them enter and at once I knew that there was something wrong. It was not the dress, it was their bearing.

To me and, I am afraid, to everyone else in the mosque, it stood out a mile. Later, I tried to explain it to Miss Nightingale.

"I hope I was not lacking in respect?"

"Indeed not, Miss Nightingale."

"Then—?"

I found it hard to say. They had stood there somehow four-square, and that was not the way women stood, not in Egypt, at any rate.

"I know what you mean, Mr Wood. My bearing was insufficiently meek."

"Well, I wouldn't quite put it like—"

"It is so, nevertheless." She was silent for a moment and then said firmly, "And I would not have it otherwise."

"I very much regret—"

"It was not your fault, Mr Wood. Nor Mr Murray's, either. You both tried to dissuade us. I brought it upon myself, although all I had wished to do was see how others worshipped and share, if I could, the joy—"

"You can hardly be blamed, my dear," said Mr Bracebridge.

He was still angry. When I had hustled them out of the mosque he had been about to confront the crowd that had accompanied them. It was Mr Murray who had, more wisely, somehow got them into a carriage and hurried them away.

"I shall complain to the Bey," he said.

"Please don't," I said.

"It is not my habit to accept affronts," he said. "And I have no fear of foreign potentates."

"That is not the point," I said.

He looked at me quickly.

"You think it a waste of time? That he will do nothing?"

"Quite the reverse," I said, "he'll have them all flogged. But is that what you want?"

He hesitated.

"It would be better to leave it," said his wife.

"Yes," said Miss Nightingale. "Leave it. In any case, I am no longer sure that the incident is to be regretted."

"Not to be regretted?" said Mr Bracebridge, bewildered.

"It was demeaning and degrading!" said Mrs Bracebridge vehemently.

Miss Nightingale put her hand on the older woman's arm.

"Yes, my dear, it was. And I am so sorry to have subjected you to it. I should have said, not entirely to be regretted. For in that quarter of an hour I learned something." She looked at me. "I learned what it is to be a woman in a country like this where Christ has not been to raise us."

It was with some relief that I escaped and went round the corner to the Hôtel d'Orient, where the French party was staying. The door was opened by Monsieur Flaubert. He was wearing a long white *galabeah* and his head had been shaved in the Muslim fashion, leaving one lock at the back of the head for Mohammed to lift him up by on the Day of Judgement.

"What on earth—"

He pirouetted, then stepped aside to show me Maxime du Camp, similarly attired, sitting cross-legged on his bed and smoking from a water pipe.

"How does it strike you?"

"Powerfully."

Fresh from my experience with Miss Nightingale, I was, however, a little worried.

"Should you have it in mind to go out like that," I said, "I would caution against it."

"Why so?"

Again I found it difficult to put into words.

"It can only confuse."

"But is not that a good thing?"

"Not here it isn't. They might feel that you were, well, mocking them."

"They have no sense of humour?"

"They have a very considerable sense of humour. Only it may differ from yours."

"I think Monsieur Wood is advising prudence," said Maxime.

"It seems, however, a great pity to come all this way and then be prudent. Besides, is it necessary? Surely, if we were attacked, the viceroy would take action?"

"He certainly would. But after the event."

"I think I am in favour of prudence," said Maxime.

It came, I suppose, out of their desire to embrace the East, whatever the East might be. One thing it might be, they made clear at once.

"We-ell," I said, "it's not quite as easy as that. The dancing girls have all been expelled."

"Expelled?"

"Yes. By decree of the viceroy."

"But why?"

"The Puritans have followed us here," said Maxime dejectedly.

"It's not just that," I said. "The fact is, the *Ghawazee* – the dancing girls – are not just dancing girls."

"Well, I was rather hoping that they wouldn't be."

"No, they're that, too, of course, but they are also thieves – gipsies – and generally disorderly."

"Perhaps we can run into them later. Meanwhile, they really have left the city?"

"I am afraid so."

"But what shall we do?"

"There are dancing boys, of course."

"And they haven't left the city? The viceroy is discriminating?"

"I could find you a troupe if you wanted."

"Well, that is something. But, do you know, tonight I feel particularly – you are sure there are no women?"

"There are always women."

There was, for example, La Triestine, in a street just behind the hotel. Not a dancing girl in the true sense

11

of the word, not a *Ghawazee*, but, as her soubriquet suggested, a European. Vaguely. Would she do? They thought she might.

I took them to the house and then would have left them but they demurred.

"They might not understand."

"Oh, I think they will."

They insisted, however, and I went up with them into what had been the harem room of the house. As was usual with such rooms, one end of it extended into a large box window which projected far out into the street until it almost touched the corresponding window on the other side. There was no glass and privacy was secured by heavy ornamental fretwork which made it possible for harem inmates to see out but prevented others from looking in. It also allowed air to pass through and made it one of the coolest parts of the house. A large divan had been placed near the window to take advantage of this.

On the opposite side of the room was another large window, this time without either glass or woodwork, open entirely to the wind, and through it one could see a solitary palm tree. Because the room was so dark, lit only by a single oil lamp, the night sky stood out clearly. Beyond the palm tree, at the other end of what seemed to be a garden, rose a minaret.

There was another divan in the room, a long, low one, covered by a mat at one end, on which a litter of kittens was lying. After a while, two women came in, sat on the divan, cross-legged, and began playing with the kittens. They were both in traditional silk robes embroidered on the front with gold, which flashed occasionally when it caught the light from the lamp. There was a flash, too, when the light caught the gold coins bound into their head-dress.

One of the women began to drum with her fingers on the wooden edge of the divan. Normally, there would have been a *darabukkeh*, a tunnel-shaped drum, but music had been forbidden in such places under the recent rules. The other woman stood up, took off her girdle, which had been covering her midriff, and knotted it low on her hips, exposing her tummy. She began to dance to the drumming, slowly at first and merely with rhythmic movements of the hands and arms, then more quickly with long, shivering movements which made the whole of her abdomen quiver.

The drumming and the dancing stopped and the two women began to remove their clothes. There was the rustle of silk and an odd, distinct chink from the coins in their head-dresses. The kittens were removed from the mat and the women were ready.

Afterwards, as we walked back to their hotel in the moonlight, the two Frenchmen discussed their experiences.

"Dry; though sufficient grease for lubrication."

"The shaving has an odd effect."

Flaubert complained of a headache. It had not been the

exercise itself, he said, but the things that had gone with it. There had been too much to take in, too many contrasts.

"Splendid things," he said, "gleamed in the dust."

He wished they had been able to talk to them. When it was over, the two women had helped them to dress, and while they were doing so, one of them had spoken in Arabic. What had she said?

I told them. They then spent more time discussing whether words added to or diminished the experience. In the end they concluded that foreign words were best for they gave the illusion of communication while denying it added to the mystery.

Flaubert, however, was still not satisfied. "There must be some communication, I think."

"There can be," said du Camp, "if you have an interpreter."

"Lovemaking by interpreter?"

They both seemed pleased by the idea.

Later, I went round to the Bosquets. I had got into the habit of doing so and went round most evenings, although not usually as late as this. Fortunately, they were still up, sitting outside in the garden, sufficiently far from the lamp as to be able to read from its light but not so close as to be affected by the insects which spun in a continuous halo round the flame.

The coffee pot was still warm on the brazier and Madame Bosquet poured me some without asking. Old

Bosquet brightened and went into the house for brandy. Aimée smiled at me and went on with her sewing. The other children were all in bed, up on the roof.

I described my day. They knew I had been expecting parties. French themselves, they were particularly interested in the Frenchmen.

"I knew they were coming," said old Bosquet. "Delaporte told me. Apparently they wish to visit the hospital."

Delaporte was the French Consul and had received messages a couple of days before from Alexandria. One of the Frenchmen, it seemed, was a doctor. Or perhaps his father was a doctor. Bosquet was in charge at the Kasr el Aini Hospital.

I told them, guardedly, how the Frenchmen had spent their evening. Old Bosquet shrugged.

"Men will be men," said Madame Bosquet equably.

Aimée put down her sewing.

"Will they?" she said. She looked at me. "I hope you will not be."

She and I were not exactly engaged but we had an understanding.

"I am reserving my energies," I said.

Old Bosquet laughed. Aimée frowned. I was never quite sure how she viewed the urgency of our relationship. The Bosquets were fond of me, I thought, but I was doubtful about how her parents would view marriage to someone whose prospects were as uncertain as my own. I had shared with them my hopes for a position with the

15

Transit Administration or perhaps in Mr Shepheard's growing hotel business and I thought they approved, but a permanent position had not yet materialised and they could be forgiven any doubts about my capacity to support a wife on my present precarious earnings as an independent agent.

Aimée, I was sure, or nearly sure, shared my belief that the passage business would grow and grow in Egypt, and also shared my confidence that I would one day find a suitable position within it. But occasionally and, lately, increasingly, I thought I detected flickers of impatience at the slow progress of our relationship.

As I walked home through the streets that night the moon was making the sand as white as snow. It was a thought I often had, not because I was always thinking of England but because Egypt's capacity to transmute ordinary things into the stuff of – well, not legend, perhaps, rather, romance, the romance of *The Arabian Nights*, still caught me as freshly as it had done five years before when I had first landed in the country.

I had been a romantic then and I was one still. It was what had brought me out to Egypt in the first place.

What had brought Mr Flaubert? I wondered. Was he a romantic, too? I thought perhaps he might be, for surely some magic must have transfigured the dumpy, red-faced Triestine and her worn companion.

And Miss Nightingale? Was she another romantic?

What had brought her to Egypt? Was it romance, pursued or fled? I feared it might be only a romance with God, which was, from my point of view, the most unsatisfactory kind since it imposed such peremptory limits on the way one saw things. I had met biblical parties before!

I wanted people to see Egypt with fresh eyes, not with the eyes that they had brought with them from Europe, which were distorted by their own preoccupations and prejudices. I expect you think I'm going to say that I wanted them to see Egypt as it really was, but that is not so. I wanted them to see the snow as well as the sand.

Two

The next morning I was at the Hôtel de l'Europe early, *very* early. Miss Nightingale appeared to be the only one up. She was sitting at a table copying out plans of temples. "I do like to see things clearly in my mind beforehand," she said, frowning at the line she had just drawn. "I know that when I actually get to the place, the detail will confuse me." She put down her pencil and turned to me with a warm smile. "Well, Mr Wood, what have you got for us this morning?"

"A visit to the Place of Tombs."

"These are not the pyramids, I presume?"

"No, no. These are the tombs of the caliphs. Much later."

"A sort of cemetery?"

"Well—"

"I like cemeteries."

"Oh, good. However—"

It was amazing how 'howevers' multiplied when Miss

Nightingale was around. There was, first, the question of the Place of Tombs itself. Cemetery, in the pallid European sense of the word, was what it was not. But how to convey that and should I attempt to convey, anyway? Would it not diminish the experience? I did not share Miss Nightingale's view that in order to best apprehend a thing, you had first to approach it in abstract.

"It is an area of funerary mosques," I said neutrally.

She stood up eagerly.

"I must arouse the others."

But I could already hear them coming down the stairs. Which brought me to the second 'however'.

Donkeys really were the best way of getting around Cairo. Its narrow medieval streets would not take carriages and walking was hardly possible for such a distance as this. The Place of Tombs was beyond the eastern edge of the city and to get to it you had to go some way out into the desert, which in the heat . . . But could they be persuaded?

They could, it seemed. The experienced Bracebridges raised no difficulty. Miss Nightingale, reassured, no doubt, by Divine precedent, was prepared.

"With an Egyptian donkey, Miss Nightingale, you sit *here*, near the tail, weight well back. You crook your leg round the saddle-horn – if you will allow me – so! No, it is a man's saddle, or rather, a *universal* saddle, men and women use it equally. No, you will not fall off. Ahmed, here, will be running beside you and he will support you

in case of need. The other side? Ah, well, there we will
have Abdul, who will perform the same service. Words
of command? Well, of course, the donkeys speak only
Arabic, but Ahmed—"

And running in front would be the *sais*, the groom,
skirts tucked up, freshly beturbaned and cracking his
whip. Which turned out to be another 'however'.

On the outward journey there was no problem. This
early in the morning the streets were empty. The bread
makers were still making their bread, and from inside
the houses you could hear the slaps as they worked. One
or two early stallholders were setting out their wares but
the chickens were still in their baskets and not running
around getting under the feet of the donkeys. Occasionally
we met a camel, its bulky load of firewood or clover
almost spanning the street, but for the most part we were
fortunate and encountered them only at junctions, where,
forewarned by the whip cracking, they usually drew aside
to let us pass.

We made good progress through the quiet, still half-
dark streets until we reached the city gates and emerged on
to the desert, which was reddening in the just-rising sun.
There I made them dismount. We took a footpath which
led up into the low mounds known as the Windmill Hills.
I would not let them lift their eyes until we reached the top,
then I brought them out on to a ridge and let them look.

It was a sight to stagger. Below them the long line of
funerary mosques, each one more fantastic than the rest,

a great, deserted city wrenched out of the Arab Middle Ages unrolled like a magic carpet before them. Dome gave on to arabesqued dome, minaret to slender minaret, arch to arch, colonnade to colonnade. Everywhere, one extraordinary shape led on to another, a kind of riot of Arabian Gothic. The sun was dying the masonry red and bringing out the blue strips round the domes, making the enamel tiles glow and sparkle. It was a vision from the Arabian Nights.

Gratified, I took them down again to the waiting donkeys. We rode on in silence. I was too experienced to allow the effect to be dissipated by surfeit so I took them to only a few individual mosques: the Kait Bey, with its loggia and steps, the fortress-like Sultan Barkuk, with its open arcades, through which I let them wander; the monastery-like El Azraf, with its college and almshouses; and the twin mosques of Sultan Inal and the Emir Kebir, so close together that they seemed like one great red building.

The doors at these last two were always kept locked, but it did not matter because there is a breach in one of the walls at the back through which the ladies could be lifted. I wanted them to see the court with its arched cloisters and the two domes at the corners, under which the tombs were lying.

Miss Nightingale dusted her skirt and looked round her.

"Even here," she said.

"I beg your pardon?"

She made a gesture with her hand.

"What creatures are these?"

From out of the ruins people came crawling.

"The poor use the mosques as dwelling places," I said.

She was silent for a little while, then said, as if to herself, "What I could do in a place like this!"

The remark was not really addressed to me and yet I felt piqued. The mosques, for me, were perfection; what could one 'do' to perfection? She was talking, I knew, about poverty and not about perfection, but in Egypt it was hard to separate them, they were both so intimately bound into the country. They were what the country *was*. Who was Miss Nightingale to feel she could take it upon herself to 'do' anything to Egypt?

"You must not see it like that," I said.

"But to be so reduced!"

"The buildings, as you can see for yourself, are dry and comfortable. They are better than many other dwellings in Egypt."

"Graves, nevertheless!"

"Not quite, Miss Nightingale. Funerary buildings."

"The associations, however—"

"Are not quite the same for Egyptians as they are for us. Cemeteries in Egypt are for the living as well as the dead. Rich families, for instance, often build a house near their tomb. They use it on the occasion of the great festivals, when they come and live in it, often for several days. The point is, they *live* in it. They rather enjoy it, the women especially. Cemeteries in Egypt are quite jolly places—" Miss Nightingale raised an eyebrow.

The incident occurred just as we were about to leave. The beggars had been unusually importunate, one boy especially, and an over-zealous policeman, observing this, rushed up, seized the boy and began to belabour him. The boy's white turban became undone and streamed upon the wind. His cries were piteous and aroused the ladies' indignation.

"Cannot you do something, Mr Wood?"

The policeman, surprised, stayed his hand. The boy scampered off. Abdul brought the donkeys and I thought the matter at an end. Miss Nightingale, however, returned to it when we were back at the hotel.

"The brutality, Mr Wood!"

"It is, alas, the custom of the country, madam."

"But should the custom be condoned?"

"We may not like it, Miss Nightingale, but I am not sure it is for us either to condone or condemn it."

"But ought we not at least to avoid practising it?"

"Well, of course—"

"And yet you, yourself, Mr Wood—"

"Oh, come, Miss Nightingale."

"But *yes*, Mr Wood!"

"No, Miss Nightingale!"

"The *sais*. Your very own – *our* very own – servant!"

"But, surely, Miss Nightingale, you have not seen—"

"He runs before us with a whip!"

"But he doesn't actually beat anybody! Much. He just cracks his whip. It is the noise, Miss Nightingale. It alerts people to our passage. It is the custom, when some great personage approaches—"

"Office, in this wretched country, is heralded with a whip?"

"It is the *noise*, Miss Nightingale, just the noise!"

She was silent for a moment. Then she said quietly, "No, it is not just the noise, Mr Wood. I have seen it. Not just today, and not just here. In Alexandria, too. Everywhere in Egypt the whip is the symbol of authority, and not just the symbol – the reality, too."

"It is too frequently resorted to," I admitted.

"I am not blaming you, Mr Wood. I understand that the previous pasha was notorious for his severity. And no doubt he was not the first. The whip is written into the history of this country, Mr Wood, the whip and the bastinado stick."

She was silent again for a little while.

"So much wretchedness!" And then, as if to herself, "And such beauty!"

I was glad she had noticed the beauty.

As we were crawling along one of the tunnels on hands and knees we met a party of Englishmen crawling the other way. Maxime raised his hat politely. After a pause, the Englishmen did likewise.

"With Englishmen it is necessary to be correct," said Maxime.

He and Flaubert were wearing hats on my advice, to guard against the bat droppings. The floor was slimy with bat dung. There were more bats in this pyramid than in the others. We could hear their sharp little cries. I had warned that this was so but Flaubert had been especially anxious to enter this one. He had read in Herodotus that it had been built on the order of Rhodopis, the famous Greek courtesan. This had pleased him immensely.

"We hear much about the power of the pharaoh," he said, "but what about the power of the prostitute? Which, fortunately, is still with us."

The pyramid is one of the smaller ones and less visited than the others. The corridors are more roughly hewn and the roofs lower. Some are half-filled with rubbish. One of the central chambers has collapsed. For some reason Flaubert elected to make this one the last dwelling place of Rhodopis. He examined it by candlelight. Overhead, the bats squeaked irritably.

Then back to the long, slippery climb out, the Arabs going ahead of us with candles to light the way, their skirts hitched up round their waists, their bare feet scrabbling on the stone, occasionally sliding back under our noses, we following on all fours. By the time we had reached the top we had had enough. The Arabs pulled us up the last bit and we emerged blinking and sweating into the sunlight.

Flaubert threw himself down on the sand in front of the Sphinx and took out his pipe. Maxime went off to his tent to fetch his photographic apparatus. He intended to take a number of photographs while he was here and so I had arranged for them to camp at the pyramids for two or three days. I myself would be able to stay only for one day because of my duties in the city, but I had appointed a reliable major-domo, hired the biggest guard I could find, and organised supplies of food from a nearby village, and thought that now they might safely be left. First, however, I wanted to observe Maxime at work.

He had told me about his mission that first night as we were walking back from La Triestine's. The French Government, he said, had entrusted him with a special task: to make a photographic record for the Académie des Inscriptions et Belles-Lettres of the monuments and inscriptions he encountered during his visit. It would be the first time, he thought, that photographs had been used for such a purpose and there would be considerable interest back in Paris in the outcome of his efforts.

"It will be so exact," he said enthusiastically. "For the first time those who cannot travel will have an opportunity of seeing objects as they really are. Hitherto they have had to rely on possibly inaccurate drawings or inadequate verbal descriptions. But what can drawings do? What, verbal description?"

"What indeed?" said Flaubert.

He was looking now at the Sphinx.

"It is," he pronounced, "definitely negroid. The lips, the ears. And the fact that the nose is missing somehow contributes to that effect. It adds to the general flatness."

"I wonder if I shall get that?" said Maxime, fussing around. "I shall get the lips and the ears, but – no, I shall get everything. Everything that is there."

"The bird droppings?" said Flaubert.

The left side of the Sphinx was white with bird droppings.

"I shall get something."

"Will you get Buffard?"

"Buffard?"

"He has written his name at the top of the Great Pyramid."

"Well, if that's where he's written it, no. I am photographing the Sphinx."

"But if he had written it there?"

"Then I would get it. If it was large enough."

"It's large to him."

"But it's not large to me. In fact, it's not even there! This Buffard is a complete irrelevance."

"Quite so. Nevertheless, he has written his name on the Great Pyramid, and the fact that he is a wallpaper manufacturer. He clearly thinks that is important."

"The man is an imbecile!"

"True. However, his name is on the pyramid. That is important."

"I don't think that is important."

"On the one hand you have the Pyramid, Great; on the other you have Buffard, wallpaper manufacturer. Isn't that important? The conjunction!"

"No. And it's not on the Sphinx, either."

"How do you know it's not? His name might be buried under the bird shit."

"The best place for it!"

"If it was, you wouldn't see it on the photograph. Your apparatus sees only what is on the surface. It does not see what is buried."

For some reason the thought seemed to cheer Flaubert up. He got to his feet and walked round the Sphinx, whistling. Maxime shrugged his shoulders and immersed himself in his apparatus. That evening, the Englishmen we had met in the pyramid paid us a visit. We entertained them with coffee, sitting on the sand in front of our tents, smoking the long pipes of the Arabs.

I had managed to hire a *dahabeeyah* from a wealthy pasha and took the Bracebridges to inspect it. The pasha had reserved it for his private use and it was larger and more sumptuously fitted out than most such boats, although a thing or two would have to be done to it before they could occupy it.

"I hope that won't take long?"

"Oh, no."

It was the normal practice when a boat was hired out to Europeans to take it first across to the other side of the river and then sink it to rid it of the vermin. I did not, however, mention this to the Bracebridges.

"I think it would suit us admirably," said Mrs Bracebridge, having looked round.

"It is, of course, a harem boat."

"Harem boat?" said Miss Nightingale.

"Family boat, I should say. It has been reserved for the private use of the pasha's family when he is travelling."

This accounted for the spacious accommodation: there were three sizeable cabins; a sitting room with green panels and a divan all round it; a large cabin for the Bracebridges; and a smaller one aft for Miss Nightingale and her maid. The cabins were above deck and occupied the after-part of the vessel, which gave it a lop-sided, top-heavy look. The hold, however, was forward to counterbalance the weight at the other end. There were two masts, a large one forward and a smaller one aft, and somewhere the *reis*, the boat's captain, and his twelve-man crew were secreted.

It was the custom, I explained to Mr Bracebridge, to register the necessary contracts with the consul, which safeguarded the interests of both parties. I would handle all that side if he wished.

"I would be most grateful."

And finally there was the question of the dragoman.

"Dragoman?"

"Interpreter. And guide and general manager. In fact, most things."

Good men were in short supply. However, I would let him have the names of some I considered suitable and arrange for them to attend for interview. Since whoever was chosen would be living at close quarters with them for some weeks, it was important that he be personally sympathetic.

Mr Bracebridge hesitated.

"I must admit that we have been hoping – well, that you yourself might consider . . ."

I will not say that the thought had not occurred to me. But if it had, it had also been rejected. The status of dragoman was less defined then than it has become since; but even in those days it was not the kind of position that you would normally find a gentleman occupying, not an English gentleman, at any rate. Some dragomans were European. Indeed, at that time it was more common for a dragoman to be a European than not. But that was not quite the same thing.

". . . if, that is, Mr Murray could spare you."

"Perhaps you could persuade him to let you take a furlough?" suggested Mrs Bracebridge.

"We would, of course, recompense you for any loss of—"

But why not? It does not do for a man who wants to make his way in business to be too conscious of his standing as a gentleman. The best men, Mr Shepheard used to say, are the men who best know their stuff. This would give me an opportunity to get to know mine. Besides, I was sure I could strike a financial bargain which would impress even the Bosquets and perhaps persuade them to look more favourably upon me as a prospective son-in-law.

"Let me add my voice, Mr Wood," said Miss Nightingale, smiling. "It would be such a pleasure to have you with us."

That was how I came to do it.

And, lastly, the Levinge. It was a contrivance recommended by Mr Wilkinson, to whose book, *Modern Egypt and Thebes*, Miss Nightingale accorded much the same authority as she did to the Bible. He recommended a number of other things, too, including a foot tub (of tin or copper), two sorts of apricots, a flag with a pulley and rope for raising it and almond paste for clarifying the water. He clearly liked his smoking for he specified not only pipes but spare mouthpieces and pipe bowls and wire (to be put into a reed) and tow for cleaning them. A practical fellow, too, he recommended stoppered earthen jars for things that rats might eat and also an iron rat trap. Together with the Levinge, which consisted of a pair of sheets sewn together at the bottom and the two sides. To the upper end was added a thin piece of muslin which served as a mosquito net, and which was drawn tight at the top by a tape or string. The whole thing was suspended from a nail and inside the muslin were threaded canes to form loops and hold the muslin out like a kind of cage. One could either sit in the cage or stretch out horizontally in the sheets on a mattress with the cage suspended over one's head like a breathing bell. In either case one was safe from small intruders.

They had acquired their Levinges in London and now swore by them.

"But you, yourself, Mr Wood?"

"I am afraid not."

"But in that case, do you not find the insects troublesome?"

"There are balances to be struck, Mrs Bracebridge. For instance, in the hot season, many people, myself included, like to sleep on the roof of their houses. The roofs are flat, as I'm sure you have noticed, and underneath the stars it is really quite delightful. You catch every breath of air. For this it is worth trading the apparent protection of the Levinge."

"And the insects?"

"One just has to bear with them."

"And does everyone take the fatalistic view that you do, Mr Wood?"

"They have no choice. One could hardly equip the whole population with Levinges."

"True. True. And yet . . ."

"What is thought Oriental fatalism, Miss Nightingale, is sometimes merely realism."

"And which—?" began Miss Nightingale, as she watched the heavy iron rat trap being brought on board.

Three

"Like," said Flaubert with satisfaction, "blocks of sugar at a grocer's."

He was referring to the ibises, stacked mummified, in their jars. To get to them we had had to drop down into a hole and then crawl along a subterranean passage. Beneath us the sand, liberally mixed with fragments of pottery, crackled sharply. Flaubert had became apprehensive. In the last part of our ride to Sakkara we had seen hundreds of scorpions and now, each time a fragment cracked, he fancied that he was kneeling on one.

"If there are any," I had said at last, exasperated, "the Arab will have frightened them away."

The Arab had looked back and grinned.

"No scorpion," he had said, and to prove it had held up his torch so that it illuminated the narrow tunnel. By its light I could see the bulky form of Maxime immediately behind him and then the slighter one of the doubting Flaubert.

34

"It's not much further," I had assured him.

The light had dimmed suddenly as the Arab turned away. I heard the scrabbling of feet and then the crackling resumed.

We had come out into a small chamber and beheld the jars piled opposite us. The Arab had taken one of the jars and broken it open. He had showed Flaubert the bird and had then stepped back and held the torch high. We saw that there were jars stacked all the way round the chamber, from the floor to the roof.

"But more, I think, than in a grocer's," said Maxime.

He took the mummy of the exposed bird and held it up against the torch so that its shadow was thrown grotesquely against one of the walls.

"Which one is that?" asked Flaubert.

"Thoth, I think," said Maxime, and pitched the bird into a corner.

He chose two of the jars and stuffed them under his arm. Flaubert did likewise. The Arab glanced at me, I nodded and he stooped back into the tunnel.

Outside, the men had lit a fire and were making coffee. They had built the fire out of some painted wooden panels they had found. Yes, they were pharaonic, I told Maxime, but there was so much of it lying around and, besides, it was all fragments. These days you hardly ever recovered a complete object from the tombs.

Maxime got to his feet and began to scout round, turning over the fragments with his foot.

"He will certainly fall into a hole," said Flaubert complacently – the ground was pitted with diggings – "and break his neck. Then we will embalm him and put him in a jar."

They had moved into a new camp at Memphis a couple of days before and had had some problems. They had sent for me urgently and I had ridden over at once. I wanted to be thought indispensable. I still had hopes of being asked to find a *dahabeeyah* for them.

I broached the subject as we rode back to Cairo together.

"We are not really intending to set out until February," said Maxime.

"That is why I raise the issue now."

Maxime looked at me quickly.

"It takes time, does it?"

"It can do. There are a lot of formalities to be gone through. The contracts have to be registered."

"Contracts!"

"For your own protection."

"Do we need to go through all that?"

"You would be wise to. You are unlikely to get a decent *dahabeeyah* otherwise."

Maxime looked vexed.

"Of course, I could do it for you if you wish."

"Could you?"

He glanced at Flaubert.

"Why not?" said Flaubert indifferently.

The last part of the ride was through green fields heavy with the fragrance of beans, but before then we had been riding through desert. Flaubert kept lagging behind us. Eventually he stopped.

"I had expected it to be," he said, puzzled, "featureless. And yet—".

He called Maxime back.

"Look!" he said.

The ground to one side was covered with small stones. The light seemed to adhere to them, coating them as with a metallic sheen so that they seemed almost ceramic. The stones were so numerous that they made the whole ground glitter. If you stared long enough, the bits of glitter ran into each other and it was as if, he said, you were looking through water.

"Could you get that," he asked Maxime, "with your photograph?"

"Well—"

"It is of the surface, you see, and yet under the surface. There is more to this surface," he said, shaking his head, "than one thinks."

We rode on. Later, though, he stopped again. He had seen a slope so white that he rubbed his eyes.

"For a moment," he said, "I thought it was snow."

Coming off the *dahabeeyah* one day, I saw a huge rat sitting on one of the ropes which tied the boat to the bank. That decided me. I told the *reis* to take it across to Roda Island at once and moor it there. If we let it lie at Bulaq, in no time all the benefits of the immersion would be lost. No doubt more livestock would come aboard at Roda, but Bulaq was a grain port where rats were both abundant and adventurous.

When the boat was safely at its new moorings I suggested that the Bracebridge Party might care to ride over and visit it, even pass a night on it before departure to familiarise themselves with the conditions and remove – or, possibly, confirm – any doubts they had. They accepted the suggestion with enthusiasm and late one afternoon we set out.

We formed quite a caravan. The Bracebridges and Miss Nightingale were on donkeys with, of course, outrunners to assist them, and in front ran the *sais*. Behind us were another three donkeys carrying our mattresses. ("In Egypt, Miss Nightingale, one carries one's mattress *with* one. It is rolled up and put away in the morning and then rolled out again at night. Why? Hygiene, Miss Nightingale. But also space. And then, Miss Nightingale, people sometimes like to change their sleeping place. In summer they often sleep on the roof. Their nomadic disposition? Well, yes. Perhaps.")

She was, however, untypically silent on the ride; so much so, that I brought my donkey alongside hers and asked her if she was, perhaps, feeling the heat. She shook her head.

"There will be more air by the river," I said encouragingly, and dropped back.

Later, when we had reached the river, I tried again. "Feeling better, Miss Nightingale?"

"I am quite well, thank you."

Her indisposition, however, was apparent to the Bracebridges, too, who were possibly more familiar with it. Mrs Bracebridge, in an effort to distract her, called on her to remark the beauty of the sunset. It *was* beautiful, too. The rapidly changing colours of the sky, the reds and yellows and bronzes, were reflected in the water; reflected and subtly changed, deepened and muted, and over on the other side of the river the pyramids caught a sudden violent tint of pink. Miss Nightingale, however, merely nodded her head perfunctorily.

I felt moved to protest.

"Come, Miss Nightingale," I said, rather cunningly, I thought, "one mustn't ride unfeeling through God's wonders."

It had the effect I desired, of rousing her, but not quite in the way I had intended.

"God's wonders, no," she said. "But whose works are these?"

She pointed to some huts on the river bank, sunk so low into the swamp that the bulrushes almost closed over their roofs. The walls had been made from the dried mud of the river bank and the roofs at one time thatched with reeds, but the roofs had been allowed to sag and rain had dissolved the clay so that the whole structure seemed to be slipping back into the mud from which it had come. As we passed, half-naked creatures came crawling out, as from underground.

"These are the Devil's works," she said.

"Oh, come, Miss Nightingale!"

"'For this is his hour,'" she quoted despondently, "'and the power of darkness'."

I couldn't think what to say and we rode on in awkward silence. She seemed to become conscious of this and gave herself a little shake.

"I should not feel like this, I know," she said, "not on such an evening. But" – she looked back at the huts – "it was not like this in Italy. There, there was poverty but the people were somehow innocent, they were like children. You felt they would grow. Here" – she hesitated – "here you almost do not recognise them as human beings, they are so – so degraded."

"They are human beings nevertheless, Miss Nightingale."

"It hardly seems possible that they can be God's work," she said in a low voice.

"Miss Nightingale, you are not seeing things as they are. These are just ordinary people. They live in poverty, it is true, extreme poverty. But their condition is, well, it is not theological, it is man-made. Something can be done about it."

She turned in her saddle and looked at me.

40

"You think so, Thomas? You really do?"

"Of course I do!"

"Of course?" she said doubtfully. Then she seemed suddenly to cheer. "Of course! Thomas, I need your simplicity, I need you to rescue me!"

She urged her donkey on, then looked back over her shoulder. "I am not always like this," she said.

I had already learned that there were two Miss Nightingales. There was the one we had seen that morning, brightly chirruping away in the Shoemakers' Bazaar over a pair of yellow slippers, turning aside to point out to Mrs Bracebridge an inner court where men were working away on inlaid tables tailoring prayer mats and saddlebags and shawls, or a coppersmith holding a beaten vessel with his toes while he chased the brim, or a scent maker sitting on his counter with his gilt bottles and ivory balls alongside him.

"Not a corner that is not a picture!" she had said then enthusiastically, pulling Mrs Bracebridge into yet another alleyway. "Now, Selina, you really *must* look at this!" Urging her to consider at least a sketch if not a whole watercolour.

That was one Miss Nightingale; and then there was this other one.

The Egyptian twilight is very brief and by the time we had reached our destination it was nearly dark. Across the water, though, we could see Roda Island. Putting her hand on my arm, Miss Nightingale, now fully recovered,

41

told me how pleased she was by what would be our point of departure. Roda Island was traditionally the place where Moses had been found by the attendants of Pharaoh's daughter and she saw in this a happy omen for our voyage.

In one of the wards, at a sign from Bosquet, the inmates stood up on their beds, raised their *galabeahs* and displayed their backsides. As we went round, each one opened his anus with his fingers to show the venereal ulcer inside.

"And all in the arse?" said Flaubert.

"In this ward, yes," said Bosquet.

"Well, there's a lesson to you!" said Flaubert, looking at Maxime.

We went on to the other wards. They had asked to see the syphilitic cases first. On our way we passed the dissecting room.

"Would monsieur . . . ?"

We glanced in. On the table was the cadaver of an Arab youth, wide open.

"Monsieur is familiar with such things?"

"Perhaps," admitted Flaubert.

"Monsieur is not himself a . . . ?"

"No." Then, relenting, he said, "My father was."

"In France?"

"At Rouen. The hospital there."

"Ah!"

"I grew up in it."

"Then you *would* be familiar."

I had been surprised when they had said that they wanted to see a hospital, although I remembered that Bosque had said something about it. But this explained it. It had been easy to arrange. Old Bosquet's duties at the Kasr el Aini were not pressing these days.

"But here is something that perhaps you will not be familiar with."

We were entering the leprosy ward. Leprosy was as common in Egypt as it was further south. There were, however, only a few patients here. Flaubert passed on to examine a man whose head was oddly ringed with flaking white skin. Bosquet stopped beside him and took him through the finer points of the disease. They both had, I thought, something of the same clinical detachment.

When we had completed the tour, Bosquet suggested an aperitif. We took it outside on a verandah overlooking the Nile. In front of us *feluccas*, with their graceful lateen sails, curved and skimmed. On the opposite bank the pyramids shimmered in a purple mist. Further along the bank on our own side we could see Roda Island, where I had been with the Bracebridge party the evening before.

"Have you been to the Island?" Bosquet asked.

"Not yet."

"The Garden is poor. But the Nilometer is interesting."

"Is there not a palace?" asked Maxime.

"You can see the Palace of Mohammed Bey."

"Mohammed Bey? The one who had his blacksmith nail horseshoes on the groom who asked him for new shoes?"

Old Bosquet laughed.

"Such is the story," he said.

We were approaching the hour of luncheon, which, I have noticed, is holy to the French. Flaubert and Maxime returned to their hotel. Old Bosquet invited me back to his house.

We found the children playing in the garden. Little Gérard looked up at me.

"Pider," he said.

"Pider?"

"He has just been watching a spider in the yard," said Aimée.

"I know a game about spiders," I said.

I showed him Incey-Wincey. I daresay the French have an equivalent but in this form it seemed to be new to him. We played it together, sitting on the grass, until a shout from the house informed us that it was lunchtime. Then he took me by the hand and led me in.

"He likes you," Aimée said.

He insisted that I sit next to him. The Bosquets dined formally, with all the little ones sitting solemnly up at table. There was no playing around. Eating was a serious business in the Bosquet household.

Afterwards, Aimée took Gérard off for his afternoon sleep; not on the roof this time but in a dark, cool inner room.

At the door she turned.

"He won't settle down," she said to me, "unless you promise to read him a story."

"Let the man have his coffee!" protested old Bosquet.

"I promise," I said.

We had eaten indoors with the shutters closed. Coffee, though, was taken outside on the verandah.

Madam Bosquet asked about the Frenchman.

"He is not a doctor," Bosquet told her.

"No?"

"His father is. Or was. At Rouen."

"Ah, he comes from Rouen?" Madame Bosquet herself came from Normandy. "You must invite them round," she said to me.

"Certainly."

Walking home, though, I was not sure that I would.

Instead, on the pretext that they would soon be leaving Cairo and that it would be a shame to miss them, I invited the Bracebridges and Miss Nightingale. It turned out to be a fortunate inspiration. Not only did Miss Nightingale speak French well, she also seemed particularly interested in medicine. At any rate, she plied old Bosquet with questions about his work at the hospital. The Bracebridges, meanwhile, discussed families with Madame Bosquet, which enabled me to have Aimée to myself for part of the evening.

"She is more handsome than I had expected," she said, with a glance at Miss Nightingale.

"Handsome?" I looked at Miss Nightingale critically. I had never quite thought of her in those terms. "Well, yes, I suppose she is. But . . . angular."

"You prefer your woman with soft edges?"

"Not exactly. In fact, I wouldn't generalise at all. My mind is given to the particular in this matter."

"But the generalisation is important. Certainly to me. Given that you will be living at close quarters with this lady for over two months."

"I don't think you need have any fears on that score," I said shortly.

"No?"

"No. She is—" I hesitated. I was going to say religious but I thought that in French that meant a nun. "Devout," I substituted.

"Ah. Devout." She looked down at her lap. I thought she might even be hiding a smile. "But this is excellent," she said. "Two months? You should come back much improved!"

"I don't know that I shall be able to stand it," I confessed.

"Well, two months is a bit long. Yes," she said, musing, "two months *is* a bit long."

I knew, or, rather, I hoped I knew, that she was

not thinking now of my relationship to Miss Nightingale.

"I shall find it long, too," I said. "I hope, though, that by the time I come back it will have put me in a position to—"

I told her again, of the difference it could make to our prospects.

"With the Frenchmen, too—"

"Ah, the Frenchmen?" Her interest seemed to quicken. "What are they like?" she asked, cutting across my flow.

"Like? Well—"

"They are not, I think, devout," she suggested, glancing down at her hands again.

"No."

"Handsome?"

"Handsome? I would not say so."

"Ah, well, that will be all right, then."

"All right?"

"They come to dine with us next week."

Madame Bosquet could evidently issue her own invitations.

She caught my eye at that moment and rose. It was the general signal for dinner. Old Bosquet took Mrs Bracebridge's arm, Madame Bosquet, Mr Bracebridge's. Which left me to take Miss Nightingale's.

Afterwards, we went out into the garden, where the moon was silvering the palm trees.

"These evenings!" said Mrs Bracebridge. "Exquisite!
One would like to take them away with one."

"Well, you can, almost," I said. "You capture so much
in your watercolours."

"Not this," she said, looking around her.

We began to talk about whether she had purchased
enough artist's materials to see her through the voyage.
On the other side of the coffee table the elder Bosquets
were deep in conversation with Mr Bracebridge; and
on the far wing of the semi-circle Aimee's head was
bent towards Miss Nightingale's and they were talking
animatedly together. I wondered what subject it was that
had so involved them.

Mrs Bracebridge was a talented amateur watercolourist,
I recognised the talent and envied it. I have always
thought how wonderful it must be to see something
and then be able to capture it in such a way as to
preserve its likeness. I had tried my hand at sketching
and flattered myself that some of the results were not
entirely without merit. But a sketch is, in the end, merely
an outline impression and in a country like Egypt, where
light and colour are so important, the result can often
seem lifeless. With this in mind, I had turned to watercolour; but here I had to admit that the outcome of my
efforts was less satisfactory. Something was lacking,
either natural skill or the expertise born of tuition and
practice.

I wondered now whether I should follow Mrs Bracebridge's example and take my watercolours with me on
the voyage. True, beside her accomplishment the modesty
of my own pretensions would be starkly exposed, but
could it be that by working beside her and over so
prolonged a period my own skill would grow? Might
not this prove the opportunity I had been seeking?

For here I must offer a confession. Along with those
dreams I had of becoming something in the hotel and
travel business was another dream, quite different: that of
earning my living as an artist. The chances of that were,
I knew, slender. Among my Cairo friends was an artist
and I knew what it took. My friend painted continually
but exhibited only occasionally and when he exhibited,
rarely sold. He was able to continue simply because he
had a small private income. Yet it was a dream I was
reluctant to surrender.

You may wonder how, acknowledging my limitations
as I did, I could even allow myself to entertain the idea.
The fact was that I believed, nevertheless, that I had
something on my side. Technique, I told myself, was not
all. That could be developed. But what art also required
was a subject and that, I felt confident, I had.

My subject would be Egypt. Now of course, it could
be said that it was a subject that had already been taken
by other men. But not, I told myself, in the same way.
My artist friend, for instance, was not exactly trying to
depict Egypt; he was working on a serious of paintings

with 'Oriental' themes. What I had in mind was something different. I wanted to reveal a country.

You will say that such an aim is not very different from the one I had set myself in acting as a guide to the Bracebridges and the Frenchmen, and that is true. I now believe that the occupations of artist and guide are very similar; creative persuasion enters into each. But that was not what I thought then. I saw the two as completely separate; and one as a remote dream which had for the moment, with Mrs Bracebridge's example and the opportunity afforded by the voyage, perhaps come closer.

And now another consideration was beginning to enter my thinking. Even I could hardly overlook my short-comings as sketcher and painter, but were there not other forms of art where the technical demands were perhaps more suited to me? In particular, what of the claims of photography, of which I was hearing so much from Maxime?

I had seen some of his photographs. There were three above all which made one think. One was of a relief on the wall of a temple, which, to my mind, justified all Maxime's claims as to the advantages of a photo-graphic record. It was clear and detailed and real in a way that a sketch could not be. The second was a photograph of the Sphinx, much liked by Flaubert, where the qualities were less those of a pictorial rec-ord than those of an artistic composition. The giant figure brooded against a background which was almost geometrical.

But the third photograph was the one that intrigued me. It was one of the first ones he had taken after his arrival in Cairo, when he was trying out his equipment. It showed Flaubert, dressed in Nubian costume, standing in a garden with houses all around. The photograph was in many ways not a good one, untidy, not well composed, but it captured detail, the fretwork of the box-like *meshrebiya* windows, for example. Above all, it gave an impression of ordinary Egyptian life, or showed, at any rate, that it could have done.

Four

Miss Nightingale had, it appeared, a headache and was unable to accompany us on the penultimate day, which did not augur well for the voyage. Was it the heat, I enquired?

"No, no," said Mr Bracebridge. He hesitated. "She is sometimes subject to these things." He hesitated again. "You must not be surprised, Mr Wood, to find that she is occasionally in low spirits. In fact," he went on confidentially, "that is in part the explanation for our being here. We hoped that it would help her to put her problems behind her."

"Change of air . . . ?"

"Exactly! Different scenery. Something entirely new. Take her out of herself. Intellectual interest – very important to a person like her. Her mind," said Mr Bracebridge, lowering his voice, "is continually working."

I deliberated for a moment. I liked to know where I was.

"Not – not hereditary, I hope?"

52

"Good heavens, no! No, no, nothing of that sort! Just – just some problems." He hesitated again. "Of – of a romantic nature."

"A disappointment?" I said, relieved. "Well, these things do take time."

"No, not, not a disappointment. The reverse, rather. An – an unwillingness on her part, natural hesitation, perhaps."

I thought I understood.

"I am sure," I said, "that out here she will soon see things differently.

In fact, Miss Nightingale appeared again in the evening. They had an engagement at Mr Murray's. He had invited a Bey and his wife and Miss Nightingale was very anxious to meet them, the lady especially. She told me all about it the next morning.

". . . and she was quite *enormously* dressed. She wore a jacket and trousers of white and gold and a turban with a diamond crescent in it about as big as the citadel. I thought for a moment I would have to borrow Selina's eyeshade . . .

". . . and then after dinner they brought round pipes, *huge* pipes, about ten feet long, positively Brobdignagian, and she tucked in like a baby into its bottle, *really* like a baby into its bottle, there was this continuous gurgling and for a moment I thought it was her, but then I realised that it was the pipes. They were water pipes, you know, only I hadn't realised that at first, their bowls were covered with sweet little petticoats . . . actually, the gurgling was the most intelligent part of the conversation . . .

". . . we all spoke in Italian. Except that the Bey, after a labour of at least half an hour, brought forth a sentence in English: 'Meess, I 'ave the honneur to present a gentleman who fizzles a great sympathie for your beauté.' "

"Well, there's nothing wrong with the sentiment, surely?" said Mrs Bracebridge.

"No, but I would prefer it to be expressed with diamonds," said Miss Nightingale gaily.

She had been disappointed to find that the Bey and his wife were not, as she had imagined, Egyptian but Italian. She had wanted to secure an invitation to visit a harem.

"The harems are all closed," I said. "The pashas are in disgrace. They have been obliged to leave town. Like the dancing girls."

"Dancing girls?"

"Yes. To the great disappointment of my French friends."

"Really?" Miss Nightingale seemed puzzled. "Well, I was not especially hoping to meet them. I had in mind more ordinary women. Perhaps on our voyage?"

"We won't find any pashas down south, Miss Nightingale. They will have headed for the Mediterranean."

"They don't have to be pashas' wives. Ordinary women will do."

"That may not be easy, Miss Nightingale," I said

cautiously. "Women in this country tend to keep out of sight."

"What about the women I saw on the river bank? Could not I approach them?"

"They are best approached through their husbands."

"But I don't want to talk to their husbands. I want to talk to them."

"But how are you going to talk to them, Miss Nightingale, when you do not speak their language? For me to do so on your behalf would be most improper. I would have to secure prior permission from their husbands. Even then I would probably not be allowed to speak to them directly. Their husbands would issue you an invitation, I would attend you while they were welcoming you, and then you would go in to see the women by yourself."

"But how would I talk to them?"

"With difficulty. The point about pashas' wives is that they tend to be more accomplished, certainly as far as speaking a foreign language is concerned, and would be able to talk to you."

"Oh!"

"I will do what I can, Miss Nightingale," I said, relenting. "I may be able to secure you an invitation somewhere along our way. Customs are adhered to less rigidly in the south."

"Perhaps you should leave it to Mr Wood, dear?" suggested Mrs Bracebridge.

Miss Nightingale inclined her head in acquiescence but still seemed to be considering the matter.

"I do not think," she said after a while, "that I would care to have to be approached through my husband. However smooth the path was made by diamonds."

"Quite right!" said Aimée, when I told her about it later in the morning.

"Well, I wasn't thinking of adopting Muslim practice," I said, assuming that she was laying down markers for our future relationship.

"The general position."

I did not understand what she meant and would have asked her, only she continued, on, I thought, a different track, "It must be difficult for someone like her. With such a terrible sense of duty."

"Duty?"

"Yes. To everyone. To parents and family. To friends. The Bracebridges, even. It makes it doubly hard, when you disagree, to do what you believe is right."

"She has done it, nevertheless," I said, thinking of what Mr Bracebridge had told me.

"Yes, I know."

"You know?" I said, surprised.

"Yes. She told me. The other night. She said that her parents had wanted it very much, that everyone had seemed to want it, and that she would have found it hard to stand out against them, only—"

"Only what?"

"She wasn't sure. Either that it was what she wanted or that it was what God wanted."

"I don't think God should come into this," I said uneasily.

I could see danger here. The Bosquets were Roman Catholics and this could yet prove a stumbling block to our plans. Old Bosquet himself was not, I thought, especially devout but Madame Bosquet certainly was and on a thing like marriage—

"Well, no. But she does. Not, perhaps, into decisions about the marriage itself but into decisions about the way we use our lives. What helped her, she said, was the realisation that she had a wider duty than just to family."

"That is all very well," I said, "but it does not do to sacrifice oneself to an abstract."

"Is God abstract? I don't know, I think she sees him embodied in the people around her and believes that by helping them she serves him. It comes back, you see, to this question of duty."

"I don't think you should press the notion of duty too far," I said.

Aimée laughed.

"You wouldn't, darling!" she said. "Not too abstract and not too far! How very British!"

She leaned forward and kissed me.

"However," she said, "I am inclined to agree with

you. There is another duty, too – the one you owe to yourself."

"Quite so!" I said, relieved.

"The trouble is," said Aimée, "that it cannot be taken on its own. It is always part of something else. Marriage, for instance."

"It can perfectly well be expressed in marriage," I said.

"Yes," said Aimée, "but the question is on what terms? So, at least, Miss Nightingale thinks."

I was beginning to think that it would be a very good thing when Miss Nightingale sailed off up the river.

Flaubert folded the letter and threw it down on the divan beside him.

"It is from my mother," he said to Maxime.

"Well, I trust?"

"Yes." He seemed vexed, however. "She is after me again," he complained.

"What is it this time?"

"The same old thing."

"Job?"

"Yes."

Maxime shrugged.

"It wouldn't suit you," he said.

"What would?" said Flaubert, getting up off the divan and beginning to pace up and down. "I hate these boring jobs!" he burst out. "They take too much out of you. You can't sell suet all day and then expect to write poetry at night!"

"My thoughts exactly," I said.

He stopped and looked at me in surprised.

"Your thoughts, young Thomas?"

"It's what I was thinking last night," I said.

"You think about art while you are currying the donkeys?"

"I think about jobs. Would you call photography a job, for instance?" I asked Maxime.

"Certainly not. It is a pursuit."

"Not more than that? If pursued with seriousness? Can it not become an art?

"Pursued with seriousness and talent," said Flaubert. "But that does not make it a job."

"I think of my mission as art," said Maxime, "but I also think of it as work. Doesn't that make it a job?"

"I think of my mission as a job," said Flaubert, "but that does not make it work."

Indeed not. I had heard about his 'mission' from Maxime. Apparently he had been asked by the French Ministry of Agriculture to collect information that might be of use to Chambers of Commerce. To the best of my knowledge, indefatigable though he was at collecting information of most kinds, this was one kind that had never engaged him. He had sought the accreditation purely in the interests of facilitating his dealings with officials and the only evidence I had ever seen of his 'mission' was the style he had instructed his mother to use on the envelopes she so frequently addressed to him: *Chargé d'une mission en Orient*, which was what, perhaps, had put it into his mind.

He used the style now, however, when signing the contract for the hire of the boat. I had brought copies round that morning, anxious to complete the arrangements before my departure with the Bracebridges the following day.

"I will lodge them with the consul before I go," I said. "You can be confident that the terms will be adhered to."

Broadly, that was. Much would depend on the dragoman. I had chosen him myself. He was a Genoese who had spent most of his life in Egypt and knew the country, and the river customs, fairly well. He had recently married a woman much younger than himself, who, Flaubert was persuaded, was eating him alive. If there was any truth in this, it showed itself possibly in his need for money, which I had used as a lever. I held back a portion of his pay against satisfactory completion of his duties and hoped that this would guarantee assiduous service.

"A deposit is customary," I said.

It wasn't, but I wanted to be sure of my commission. I would collect commission, too, from the man who was hiring out the boat but this would have to wait for my return.

The Dragoman's Story

Maxime wrote out a bankers' order without demur.

"And finally," I said, putting the draft in my pocket, "there are just one or two things I would like to go through with you . . ."

I went through them with Maxime. Flaubert held himself aloof from all this kind of detail. He sat waiting impatiently on the divan. From time to time he would pick up his mother's letter, glance at it, then throw it down again.

At last we were finished. Maxime looked at Flaubert.

"Yes, Right, then, young Thom-ass, let us go for lunch."

They took me, since this was our last day together (until, I hoped, their return), to a Turkish restaurant. As was his custom, Flaubert wrote down the list of dishes. He then, however, summoned the chef and enquired after the ingredients of each separate dish, which he also wrote down. I was all for knowledge, indeed, for recording knowledge, as it is an excellent way of fixing it in your mind, but surely this was going too far. What could possibly be its point?

I had, of course, remarked upon his habit before. Everywhere we went he would take out his notebook and everything I told him he would write down. At first I had found it flattering. One likes to have one's bons mots recorded, after all, and I thoroughly approved of his seriousness. Into his notebook went details of all the mosques we visited: El Hakim, with its minarets like

Ancient Egyptian pylons; Ibn Tulun, with its remarkable Arab plaster work; the Merdani, with its Saracenic battlements and windows; the Ibrahim Agha, with its blue tiles; the ruined El Amr; the Sultan Hassan, so beautiful that, according to legend, the right hand of its architect was cut off so that he would never be able to repeat his work and it would remain the finest building in the world ("Now just be careful with those photographs," Flaubert had warned Maxime. "Don't make them too good!"); El Azhar, with its rows of columns, a teacher at the base of each, with the students sitting round with their slates of tin or of yellow wood. Into it went descriptions of the Old Gates and of the Citadel, of Saladin's aqueduct and the Ders of Old Babylon, of the fountain, houses and fortresses . . . I regarded him, all in all, as a model tourist.

Even to me, however, he seemed sometimes to carry things to excess. In the Scentmakers' Bazaar, for instance, with its rows of cupboard-like shops and the owners sitting on the counters with their phials and vials spread out beside them, he had spent hours making a list of all the perfumes, oils and pomades. When a wedding procession passed us in the street he ran along beside the camels listing all the ornaments they wore.

Maxime and he even went to the lengths of hiring a man to come and give them lessons on Muslim duties and customs: the pilgrimage to Mecca, birth, circumcision, marriage rites and death rites with the final questioning by the examining angels. Maxime told me he had in mind writing a book on Muslim ways and customs. But what had Flaubert in mind?

Without some purpose in mind, this perpetual, indiscriminate collecting of information was bizarre. I wondered now, sitting in the Turkish restaurant and watching him make his lists, whether his relentless activity was not in some way connected with the issue his mother's letter had raised. Was it perhaps a way of crowding out doubts about the apparent lack of purpose in his life? Certainly, the letter seemed to have touched him on the raw, calling back into question some major choice that confronted him.

Was I, perhaps, not the only person to have vocational doubts?

"We have brought our gimlets with us," announced Miss Nightingale brightly.

"I beg your pardon?"

"Gimlets."

She showed me.

"Yes . . . but *why* have you brought your gimlets?"

"To hang things on."

"Well, there are hooks already."

"And act as pegs for doors where there are no fastenings."

"Very useful, I am sure."

"And a hundred and one other things. So Miss Martineau says."

"Miss Martineau?

"She made this journey two or three years ago. And wrote a book about it."

"I see. Well, very practical, no doubt."

Less practical were the other things they had brought. A long line of donkeys stretched along the river bank. Trunks, portmanteaux, boxes, baskets, chests and bags loomed apparently to infinity.

The *reis* looked at me.

"We may have difficulty stowing all those, Mr Bracebridge," I said.

"Could they not go in the hold?"

"Much has already gone in the hold. I am afraid that these will have to encroach on your living space."

"Could they not go on the deck for the time being?"

"I am afraid that much of the space has already been earmarked."

The crew were manoeuvring a large hen-coop on to the prow.

"Those boxes . . ."

Two large boxes, each about six feet by four, blocked off the front of the boat.

"For our provisions, Mr Bracebridge."

Also for our provisions were baskets hanging from overhead lines and from the roof of the kitchen, and cages for the meat, likewise suspended against the rats.

The kitchen was another box, of about the same dimensions as the others only tilted on end.

"Perhaps between the kitchen and the boxes?" said Mr Bracebridge despairingly.

"Fuel, Mr Bracebridge. That is where the cook will keep his fuel. And then, of course, there is the *goullel*."

"*Goullel?*"

"For the water. It is where the water is filtered."

And now on the bank there was a disturbance. Another line of donkeys came into view, each one with baskets on its back. From inside the baskets came squawking and clucking.

"Surely . . ." began Mr Bracebridge.

"They will go in the *felucca*," I said, reassuringly.

Behind us we would be towing a small sailing boat to assist us in getting ashore when the *dahabeeyah* was moored in mid-stream, and for smaller expeditions.

"Is that a goat?" said Miss Nightingale, joining us.

It was, legs tied and slung across a donkey's back. It, too, would go in the *felucca*, as would a large flock of pigeons. The pigeons would be left to roam loose and would make no attempt to fly away.

Lastly, there was a cat, which would *not* go in the *felucca* but would make its home in the *dahabeeyah*, where, it was hoped, it would keep the vermin down, or at least fight to an honourable draw.

Loading continued for the rest of the afternoon, which meant that the passengers were unable to take a siesta. Instead, they remained in their cabins and saw to the stowing of their baggage. The Bracebridges had the

Michael Pearce

front cabin, next to the sitting room. Then came a short passageway with closets, in one of which I kept my few possessions (I would sleep outside, as was my custom, up on the roof), and then there was the small cabin of Miss Nightingale.

And Trout.

"Trout?" said Aimée, when I went to take my farewell that evening. "What is this – a fishing expedition?"

Trout was the name of Miss Nightingale's maid. At least, that was what Miss Nightingale called her. I never plucked up enough courage to ask if that was her real name. Nor did I have quite enough confidence to address her by it, which somewhat inhibited our intercourse – that and the fact that she was by nature a quiet, withdrawing sort of woman, pleasant enough but not a person you would be conscious of in company.

And middle-aged, I hastened to assure Aimée.

"That comes as some relief," said Aimée. "I was beginning to think that you were taking a harem with you."

"Far from it," I said. "In so far as I have a harem, I am leaving it behind."

She continued to affect concern over so long a proximity to Miss Nightingale. While most of it, of course, was raillery, I thought I detected an undercurrent of genuine anxiety, with which I was not dissatisfied; although how she reconciled her fears with the picture she had so recently given me of Miss Nightingale as a duty-loving, God-fearing Christian paragon was not entirely clear.

66

That Miss Nightingale had her dangers, I could believe; but I suspected they were more to Aimée than they were to me.

I could not stay long, but before I left I hinted that when I returned, my improved prospects would surely encourage the family to view favourably a certain proposition that I would be putting to them.

Old Bosquet laughed.

"We shall see, we shall see."

Madame Bosquet said nothing.

By the time I got back to the boat the loading had finished. The Bracebridges and Miss Nightingale were sitting up on the raised upper deck which would serve them as a kind of open-air drawing room for the duration of the voyage. They invited me up to join them.

"All set, Mr Wood?"

"Very nearly all set," I replied, glancing along the deck. All now was still. From the kitchen came whiffs of woodsmoke.

I glanced at my watch.

"Dinner will not be served till eight. May I venture to propose a walk on the Island?"

I took them to the southern tip of the Island, which offers, in my opinion, the finest view of the Nile in all Cairo. Before us, huge *gyassas* were flying up the river, their great brown sails spread to take advantage of the evening breeze.

"The prevailing wind, Miss Nightingale, is usually from

the north, which means that we will have it behind us as we proceed up river. The current, of course, is from the south, which means that it will aid us on our return journey."

"Do not they sometimes cancel each other out?"

"They do, but the wind is intermittent, of course. The trick for the boatman is to take appropriate advantage of each."

"We must pray, then, for a following wind tomorrow?"

"That is exactly what we will do. Before we start, the crew will gather in prayer, not just for a favourable wind but for God's help throughout the whole of our voyage."

"A lesson to us all," Miss Nightingale murmured.

I pointed out to them the waterfront at Giza with its jumble of wharves and boats and the fishermen spreading out their nets to dry, and then, on the opposite side of the river, the *cangias*, those smaller cousins of the *dahabeeyah*, moored to the bank, and we watched for some time, while the sky first reddened and then darkened, the *feluccas* skimming and swooping.

Immediately below us, at the end of the Island, was a shoal, which, Mr Bracebridge conjectured, might have been the very one which the infant Moses had been cast up upon.

"The most favoured by tradition," I said, "is at the other end of the Island, opposite the Kasr el Aini Hospital."

The Dragoman's Story

Miss Nightingale asked if we could go there. I led them back first through some massive sunt trees covered with little feathery tufts of yellow blossom and then through some deserted gardens, where Miss Nightingale picked some roses and exclaimed at the poinsettia, which in Egypt grows to a height of twenty feet and bears blossoms of a size and colour unknown in England.

We walked on through bulrushes which were soon head high so that all we could see was the clear night sky above us and then we came out suddenly on the bank opposite the hospital. I pointed out to them the tree which allegedly marked the spot and we walked down to the water's edge. The reeds were full of frogs which croaked deafeningly. Opposite us the moon was just beginning to turn the palm trees silver. We stook there quietly for several moments and then Miss Nightingale took some of the roses she had plucked and threw them into the water.

"For Moses," she said.

Five

"There!" said Miss Nightingale, showing me the material she had been working on. "What do you think of that?"

"Very fine, Miss Nightingale."

It was a large piece of blue bunting with swallow tails and a red cross. On it, in Greek letters of large, white tape, was stitched the word *Parthenope*.

"You managed to find some tape after all?"

"Of a sort. Can you guess where this comes from?"

"It looks familiar," I said, inspecting it.

"I hope not, Mr Wood! It comes from my petticoats."

I was covered in confusion. Miss Nightingale laughed merrily.

"What a tribute to sisterly affection!" she said.

"Parthenope is the name of your sister?"

"Yes. And, for the duration of the voyage, of the boat."

She and Mrs Bracebridge had been working all morning. Mrs Bracebridge now showed me the fruit of her labours, too.

The Dragoman's Story

"The Bracebridge colours," she said.

The ship's *reis* took them and hoisted them into the rigging. Miss Nightingale's pennant, however, was given pride of place at the yardarm.

The wind caught them and lifted them at once. For the past three days, ever since the first morning, in fact, there had been very little wind and the men had been obliged to resort to tracking: they had paid a rope out on to the bank and set themselves to towing the *dahabeeyah* like barge horses. It was, as I pointed out, a method used on the river since time immemorial, which did not, Miss Nightingale observed, make it any the less hard work. Progress had been slow and it was only this morning, when a breeze had sprung up, that the Citadel on its eminence had finally disappeared from view. Now the sails were creaking in the wind and the boat was bounding along, inspiring the ladies to believe that the voyage had truly begun and that they really must do something about those flags.

Already the days were settling into a rhythm. In the mornings from my position on the top deck I would hear the cook begin to stir and shortly afterwards would catch the smell of woodsmoke. The crew would rise and perform their ablutions, dipping their hands over the side of the *felucca* to scoop water over their faces. They would then assemble on the main deck of the *dahabeeyah* for prayer, prostrating themselves so that their foreheads touched the boards, or sitting back on their heels, their hands crossed on their breasts, their

71

eyes looking raptly into space, while they recited the first chapter of the Koran.

The Bracebridges would say prayers too, but that was after hot water had been taken to their cabins and they had completed their toilettes. I myself shaved from a bowl on the top deck, watching the sun come up in a red ball over the edge of the desert and the first people stirring among the palm trees on the bank.

Breakfast was taken in the main cabin – grapefruit, eggs, or fish straight from the river, and toast – and then we would go up on to the top deck, where by now an awning had been raised. We would sit up there for the rest of the morning, writing letters, reading or, as I preferred to do, simply watching the river banks slip past. The banks were hardly busy yet there was always something to see: a man riding by among the palms on a donkey, women coming down to the river with jars on their heads, water buffalo paddling in the shoals, men bent working in the fields, the occasional mean houses with children playing in the water looking up to see the *dahabeeyah* pass. From time to time, further back among the palms, one would see the tops of pigeon houses poking above the trees or, more rarely, the minaret of a mosque. Always there were birds: ibises on the sandbanks, fish eagles following the line of the river, doves in the palms. When you came close to the banks the twittering of the sparrows was quite overwhelming.

Towards noon, even under the awning, it would become

so hot that most of us would retreat below. We would take luncheon at one – soup, salad, stuffed egg plants and fruit – and then the others would retire for their siesta. It is a custom I have never been able to adopt myself and I would return to the top deck where, even if there was not the deep shade that the cabins afforded, there was, to my mind, a corresponding largeness of air.

Towards four the others would come up to join me. The cook would bring us afternoon tea and, unless we were calling in somewhere, we would stay up there until the *reis* moored for the night.

In that first week we called at only a few places. The *reis* was anxious to get us up to Luxor, where the sightseeing would truly begin. In any case it was the custom to save most of one's sightseeing for the return journey, when one could be sure of the current and less at the mercy of the vagaries of the wind.

We usually moored early and in the hour or so before sunset those among us who were actively inclined would go for a walk. The party nearly always included Miss Nightingale. The crew very soon noticed this propensity in her.

"They call you 'the wild ass of the desert', Miss Nightingale."

"Not referring to my obstinacy, I hope?"

"Referring to the unbridled nature of your character," said Mr Bracebridge, with, I thought, more than his usual acuity.

"I shall take it as a compliment," announced Miss Nightingale. "Until I am the subject of an even more flattering comparison!"

I was afraid that her eagerness for perambulation indicated that she was finding the *dahabeeyah* confining.

"Not at all!" she said, surprised. "It is just that I like to get out and see things."

I knew she was impatient to reach Luxor and commence what she regarded as the real business of sightseeing. What she had come to Egypt to see were the old pharaonic temples. I was very happy for her to do that, although I wanted her to see a little more, too, but I felt for that an adjustment of approach was necessary.

The fact was that the slowness of our start was exactly what I would have wished. To understand Egypt, I believed, it was necessary to enter into her rhythms. They were not those of Europe. They were longer and slower, the rhythms of the river and the seasons, not the seasons in our sense but in the sense of Africa, with its periods of rain and its periods of drought. That was where you had to start. To come to Egypt and to fret, for instance, about the tracking – I looked accusingly at Miss Nightingale – or to talk, as some people did – I shifted my glance to Mr Bracebridge – of importing new methods of steam transport, was beside the point. Greater speed would not give greater access. In order to see Egypt, you had to slow down. Time was different in Egypt.

"We have certainly noticed that!" said Mrs Bracebridge.

The Dragoman's Story

"People here seem to have no sense of time what-soever!"

I felt that she had not entirely taken my point.

"What is special about Egypt," I said sternly, "is that here the past is not past. It is all around us. It is incorporated in the present."

"Yes, indeed!" said Mr Bracebridge enthusiastically.

I cast around desperately. Then—

"You see that *shaduf*?" I said, with sudden inspiration.

"*Shaduf*?"

I pointed. All along the banks you would see them. They consisted of a long wooden pole poised like a see-saw across a prop. To the landward end of the pole was attached a weight, usually a large ball of clay. To the other end was attached a wooden or goatskin bucket. The man working the *shaduf* would grasp the rope by which the bucket was attached and bow down, thus dipping the bucket into the water. He would let it fill and then stand back. The bucket would rise under the influence of the counterweight, usually until it reached a trough higher up the bank. It would strike the edge of the trough, tilt and deposit its contents. As it swung up again, the man would catch the rope and repeat the process. When the bank was high and the water level low, there would sometimes be as many as three sha*dufs*, one above the other, lifting water out of the river. From the topmost trough through a wooden pipe and along ditches the water would feed into the fields.

75

"A pump," said Mr Bracebridge.

"Exactly! But one that has existed since the time of the pharaohs. You will see pictures of it in the tombs that we shall visit in Thebes. It is not past," I said, "it is not present. Or, rather, it is both past and present. It is," I said, "the eternal Egypt."

That was not a word I should have used with Miss Nightingale around.

"I think I see what Mr Wood is saying," she said thoughtfully. "He is reminding us that here we can go back in time. The Old Testament is all about us. But we shall not see it unless we look in the right way."

Which was not, not quite what I had meant.

The next morning I was up, as was my custom, early, when Miss Nightingale came up on deck.

"Is there time, do you think, to go for a walk?"

"I would have thought so. There is very little wind today so we shall have to track. The men will be in no hurry to start. And breakfast can be taken whenever we return."

On the river it was still dark. Without the sun it was distinctly cold and Miss Nightingale returned to her cabin to fetch a wrap. The gangplank, as I put it out, seemed even to have a touch of hoar frost. Under the palm trees, though, it was warmer and then, as the sun rose, the pigeons began to stir and the lizards to skitter. We walked past some patches of fuzzy-headed *durra* and then saw, above some *lebbeck* trees, the tops of pigeon towers which signalled a village.

As we approached it, we met some children on their way to the river to fetch water with large jars balanced on their heads. Then we saw a woman leading out her flock, black goats and white sheep, to a shallow pool left by the inundation.

"Like Rebecca," said Miss Nightingale.

Just before the village we came to a brick field, where the mud bricks were lying out in rows to bake in the sun.

"No bricks," I said lightly, "without straw!" and showed her the chopped stalks in the mud. I had not intended a biblical reference – indeed, I had not known it *was* a biblical reference – but Miss Nightingale nodded her head approvingly.

"The task of the Hebrews," she said.

As we continued on towards the village, she seemed to be thinking.

"It is as you said. The past *is* all around us. If we have but eyes to see."

"The materials are so cheaply available," I said, "straw from the fields, mud from the river. The sun does the rest."

"God provides," said Miss Nightingale.

"Well, yes. You could say that. Yes."

We walked on. At the outskirts of the village was a large *khan*. We looked into the courtyard and saw the camels lying round the walls. Some men were sitting talking on a stone bench. They looked up as we passed. Miss Nightingale hastily pulled her wrap across her face.

The walls of the *khan* had crumbled away in parts.

"That's the disadvantage of mud as a material," I said. "When it gets a lot of heavy rain, it tends to dissolve."

"And then the house falls down?"

"The bricks melt and run into each other and become a sort of grey mess. Then the sun comes out again and bakes it hard, so that you still have something there, but it has lost its original shape."

"Like that?"

She pointed to what appeared to be a pen of some kind. All traces of the individual bricks had disappeared and what was left was a smudged, bulging mass which had sunk in upon itself. As it had shrunk, it had pulled the roof down so that it was now only some four feet above the ground. Miss Nightingale peeped in at the door.

"Sheep," she said.

A white hen ran out.

She looked again, and then shrank back.

"People!" she said incredulously. "In there! With the animals!"

A woman came out carrying a baby. Normally, Miss Nightingale would have greeted them with a smile. Now she turned away in shock and aversion.

The village was a poor one but not all the houses were as bad as that. They had clearly been built some time ago, though, and nearly all of them showed the effects of time and rain: walls were crumbling, roofs sagged and in many cases they had holes, which had been roughly covered with reeds. On some of the roofs lay dogs, which jumped down and worried us as we passed. I called to some men to chase them off but they looked at us sullenly and made only half-hearted attempts to do so.

I could not understand their response. The apathy bred by want I knew, but this was most unlike any Egyptian village I had previously encountered. In any normal village, the children would have come rushing forward. Here, they huddled in the doorways and looked at us with great round eyes, until their mothers came and pulled them back into the darkness of the huts.

At the far end of the village were the pigeon houses which we had noticed earlier. They consisted of tall brick cones into the tops of which dozens of clay pots had been embedded with their open mouths facing outwards. As we watched, some pigeons emerged and flew away down to the palm trees by the river.

"The pigeons are better lodged than the people," said Miss Nightingale.

We began to retrace our footsteps. The people, as before, shied away from us. I expressed my puzzlement to Miss Nightingale.

"It is the natural response of wretchedness," she said.

But then, riding across the fields, I saw a troop of soldiers.

"I fear there may be a more particular explanation," I said.

Miss Nightingale saw them too.

"Have those men been here?" she demanded.

"I suspect so."

"What would they have done?"

What would they have done? Well, they had not burned the village and they had not massacred its inhabitants, so the offence must have been a slight one. The Ottoman Governor's men had a way with them. But they would have been instructed to make the area safe for travellers, especially European ones, and in carrying out that task they would not have bothered with looking for individual wrongdoers, they would have made the community responsible and bastinadoed the whole village.

"Well—"

But I did not need to answer.

"The whip," said Miss Nightingale. We carried on for a little way and then she burst out, "What a wretched country this is! And what poor, wretched people!"

In the *khan* the men were still sitting on their stone bench, only now they were drinking coffee. The rich, bitter aroma reached out to us as we passed. Miss Nightingale covered her face and we hurried on, anxious to put the place behind us.

Suddenly we heard footsteps coming after us. Miss Nightingale gasped and put her hand on my arm. I turned round. A man was bringing us a tray, on which were two thimblefuls of black Turkish coffee.

"They are offering us hospitality, Miss Nightingale. We are their guests, you see."

The river's contours change all the time. New sandbanks are for ever appearing and the current is continually scooping out new headlands and bays. Sometimes when a new sandbank appears, the local fishermen mark it out with stakes. Often they plant it out with vegetables or flowers so that there, incongruously, in the middle of the river, you suddenly see a patch of onions or a bed of marvellous lupins.

The fishermen's boats are always busy among the sandbanks and islands. They are flat bottomed and so can float in a few inches of water. Every now and then you are astonished to see a man get out of his boat and walk, apparently along the surface of the water but actually on a sandbank just beneath.

Sometimes you see the fishermen standing up in their boats and beating the water with their paddle. Mr Bracebridge thought that this might be a way of propelling the boat and demonstrated vigorously how this might be done, but I persuaded him of the true explanation, which was that they were driving the fish into their nets. We saw some men laying out the nets, long, twenty-yard stretches about a yard or a yard and a half in depth, pegged out again between long stakes.

It was, I pointed out, a method which had served the fishermen of the Nile for millennia.

Sometimes, bigger boats pushed out from the bank, ferrying people with animals or vegetables to the other side. These boats were not slender-hulled and gracefully sailed like *feluccas* but broad-beamed, so broad that they wallowed through the water and seemed continually in danger of tipping their contents over the side. They had a little patchwork sail of brown cloth which hardly seemed big enough to drive the boat.

Occasionally, we saw larger vessels, a *cangia*, or a *dahabeeyah* like ours, coming down with the current, carrying a cargo of wood, stone or staves. Once or twice we met a *dahabeeyah* crowded with pilgrims, who rushed to the side and watched us as we passed.

Mr Bracebridge asked if there was a rule of passage on the river as there was on the road in England. I said that there wasn't or, at least, not one quite like that. Boats coming down the river would normally keep to the current, whereas boats going up the river naturally preferred not to encounter the current at its strongest. The river was wide enough to accommodate both. For most of its length it was between a quarter and half a mile wide, although sometimes the effective channel of passage was narrower than that because of sandbanks and shoals near the sides, which made it especially difficult for boats going up the river when there was a need for tracking.

"What do they do then?" Miss Nightingale asked.

"That depends. If the terrain is suitable for towing on the other bank then they cross to that side. Otherwise, they just have to wait for a wind."

"That is when steam would be useful," observed Mr Bracebridge.

"It would, indeed," I said. "However, there are other considerations. When the water level drops, as it does very considerably in the dry season, new sandbanks constantly appear, sometimes overnight, and it is very easy to run aground. It happens all the time," I said. "That is, I believe, why the large boats that use the river regularly tend to have their weight at the back."

"It is easy to overlook the knowledge embodied in ordinary artefacts," said Mrs Bracebridge.

"And the knowledge that ordinary people possess," said Miss Nightingale. "Think of the fishermen here!"

"They have to know the river like the back of their hand," I said.

"People speak of Our Lord as a simple fisherman," said Miss Nightingale, "but the life of a fisherman, even on the Sea of Galilee, must have been anything but simple. The River Nile is not the Sea of Galilee, I know, but He must have led a life very like this. To see them is to see Him."

Them, I was beginning to think, would have been enough.

* * *

It was true, though, that many apparently ordinary things incorporated knowledge that the casual observer was not always conscious of. When, for instance, the Bosquets' gardener wished to water the garden he would make use of an intricate system of raised ditches. He would pour water into one end and let it flow through the ditches until all were full. Then he would open breaches at various points and let the water spread over the flower beds and lawn. It was essentially the same system as the *fellahin* used to water their fields and drew on techniques of irrigation that had been developed over generations, if not millennia.

When the water was released over the lawn it would stand for some minutes in a great shallow puddle in which the Bosquet children loved to play. They would take off their shoes and stockings and stand in the water like storks. If they stood quietly enough, birds would come down to join them. Bulbuls would scoop water frantically over their backs, bee-eaters, lemon-yellow, green and chestnut-brown, would skim just above the surface snapping up insects and, if one was lucky, hoopoes, with their tall, golden, feather crowns, would stalk majestically out into the pool.

One afternoon I arrived when the children were paddling and little Gérard summoned me to join him. I removed my shoes, rolled up my trousers and walked across the water which was warm over my feet. He had found a cricket lying on a branch. We picked it up and set it on a leaf and then sent it for a voyage of navigation around the lawn. Aimée found us some time later still playing happily.

"Like children at the seaside," she informed her parents; although what that meant to her, I wasn't sure. She had been born in Egypt and had never seen a seaside, unless you count the coast of Alexandria, which is not, to my mind, at all the same thing.

For the last two days the desert had been closing in on the eastern bank. It was flat on both sides of the river but on the western side it had remained green, with a narrow strip of palm trees and the occasional village. On the eastern side there was nothing but sand. It was most inhospitable, but the presence of sandbanks across the river obliged us to moor on that side. Then the wind failed. There was a strong current at that point and the men were disinclined to track, so for two days we remained where we were.

I took Mr Bracebridge across to the sandbanks on the other side, the men rowing us in the *felucca*, where he was able to do some shooting. There were sand grouse in plenty and he was perfectly happy. The ladies were less so and on the second day I took them for an excursion to some limestone cliffs which we could see across the desert and where the men said there was an ancient quarry.

We found the quarry and it was, indeed, not without its interest – there was an ancient propylaeum there, hewn out of the rock and standing free against the cliff

– but in the heat the expedition was a mistake. The cliffs were further inland than we had supposed and the ladies became greatly fatigued. When we returned they went straight down to their cabins and did not emerge until the evening. Mrs Bracebridge soon went below again but Miss Nightingale stayed up alone on the top deck long after it had become dark.

I became concerned about her and went up.

"Miss Nightingale? Are you all right?"

She gave a little start and turned towards me.

"I am afraid we may have overdone things today. I blame myself."

"No, no."

"The heat—"

"It was not that."

"The desert can be an oppressive place."

"We experienced it only as it was."

She seemed to want to talk so I offered her my arm and we took a little turn about the deck.

"I have been trying to imagine—" She broke off and started again. "The desert is where mystics traditionally go. It is where Our Lord went before beginning his ministry. Why is that, do you think? I think it is because in the desert everything is stripped away, there is only the sky above you and the desert around." She was silent for a moment and then continued in a whisper, "It is a terrible place, Thomas. What is so terrible about it is not the absence of life but – but the denial of life. There is the sky above with its life-giving light and – and the desert resists it. It laughs at it, denies it, not thrice but a hundred times, more than a hundred times, for all eternity . . ." Her voice trailed away.

She began again. "That is why they go out into the desert, Thomas. Because there they can see more truly. There is nothing to get in the way. There is only the sky and the desert, God and the Devil."

"Miss Nightingale—"

"That is what I saw today, Thomas. God and the Devil."

"You were fatigued."

"No, no. It is as you have been telling us, Thomas: one has to learn to look with eyes that see. Today I saw." She gave a little shiver. "I realise now," she said, "that it is what I see everywhere in Egypt. I saw it in that village the other day: God's struggle against the Devil."

I was dismayed.

"Miss Nightingale, it was very exhausting. You were not yourself; *are* not yourself."

"I do not know any longer what my self is," she said despondently, then gathered herself determinedly, "But I know what I saw."

"Miss Nightingale, reflect. What you take for absolutes may not be so. There is a sky in England, too, but it is not this sky. And there is no desert below. What there is is an earth where there is life—"

She turned to me quickly.

"Yes!"

"A life that people share."

"Yes! Yes, you are right, Thomas. But I am right, too. If you go into the desert, that is what you do see. It is what Our Lord saw, what the mystics saw. That is why the great religions have begun here. And why they have not begun in England. Our skies are gentler skies. They do not insist on themselves, and so we are conscious of the earth, an earth that is gentler, too. The desert breeds mystics, our Europe produces people who are of the earth, practical, warm people – you are like that, Thomas."

"And you, Miss Nightingale?"

She was silent for a long time.

"I do not know," she said at last, with a long shudder. "I do not know."

The wind returned and we resumed our journey. Ahead of us, low against the horizon, we could see a range of yellow cliffs. Gradually the sand on the eastern bank gave way to rock, black and shiny where it was rubbed by the water. We could see now that the cliffs in the distance were a continuation of this rock and that the reason why they seemed to stretch across our paths was that the river took a great bend. In the middle of the afternoon, when everyone else was below, the *reis* pointed out to me a dark speck on top of the cliffs which he told me was the Convent of the Pulley. By the time the others came up we could see it clearly.

The Dragoman's Story

Throughout the afternoon the rocks were becoming steeper, until they turned into great imposing cliffs. Beneath the convent we could see rock staircases going down into the water.

One of the crew now appeared dressed in white English sail trousers, a blue waistcoat and a battered straw hat and equipped with a mallet.

"What is this for, Mr Wood?"

"It is a traditional ceremony, Miss Nightingale. Rather like crossing the line."

I pointed. Across the river we could see men running down from the convent and jumping into the water. Soon we could see a line of dark heads approaching. The *reis* slowed the boat and in a moment it was surrounded. We now saw the point of the mallet, for as each man tried to climb up into the boat, the crewman would run round and hit him, driving him back into the water.

It was rough fun but not as rough as it normally would have been. I had told the *reis* beforehand that I wanted the decencies preserved, and so the crew did not urinate on the swimmers as they would otherwise have done. The swimmers were Copts and the crew Muslims.

The game continued for a few moments, with the swimmers making feints and the man with the mallet rushing round, and then two of the Copts climbed up into the small *felucca* we were towing behind. We could see them standing there naked, with their long black hair trailing down behind their backs. Then the crew, fearing for their chickens, shouted the alarm and the man with the mallet jumped into the *felucca* and drove them over the side.

The swimmers now clung on to the boat and no longer made any attempts to climb on board. The man with the mallet went round and, as each swimmer opened his mouth, wedged a coin between his teeth. As soon as each man had received his money he slipped back into the water and made for the shore. We watched them land and make their way, naked, back up to the convent.

"They are, you see, monks."

"Monks?"

"That is a Christian convent, Miss Nightingale."

Six

"They have beards, you see," said Mr Bracebridge.
"They are not Egyptians, I agree," said Mrs Bracebridge, "but is that enough to make them Joseph's brothers?"

"Wilkinson is clear that the tomb is of Joseph's time," said Miss Nightingale.

"But according to Bunsen—"

We were standing before the famous picture of the procession. On the right is a large figure accompanied by what seems to be one of his sons, an attendant, and three dogs. In front of him are four rows of figures, of which the first has been described since Champollion's time as 'The Procession'. It consists of thirty-seven persons, who are being presented to the large figure by a royal scribe carrying a papyrus in his hand. Behind him stands an official and behind him the leader of the visitors. The leader and all the men of the party have beards, which made them, according to Miss Nightingale, and Wilkinson, Syrian, or at least from an area in the east. Both

91

men and women are dressed in multi-coloured garments
– the colours are still plainly visible – which was what
had led Champollion, earlier in the century, to identify
the party as Joseph's brethren.

"But, surely, it was only Joseph who had the coat?"
said Miss Nightingale.

"Not necessarily. They could all have had coats of
many colours. It may just have been that his was exceptionally so."

"Certainly there is no suggestion in Genesis that Joseph
is breaking entirely new ground," said Mr Bracebridge.
"It could, as you say, be just a question of degree. In
which case his brothers could have had many-coloured
garments too, as the figures have here. That surely sup-
ports Champollion's arguments."

"Miss Martineau, however," said Mrs Bracebridge,
glancing at the book she carried with her, "is confident."

"Miss Martineau always is," said Miss Nightingale
tartly.

I was becoming impatient at this preoccupation with
the biblical.

"But are you not missing the point? The point is,
surely, that all around us are depicted the lives of people
living four thousand years ago. Is not that something to
treasure?"

I held the torch up so that they could see the paintings better.

"Here," I said, "are people baking, weaving, washing

clothes, building boats" – I followed the wall round – "ploughing the fields, sowing, reaping, treading the corn, gathering the grapes—"

"Oh, there is one of a carpenter," said Mrs Bracebridge. "It could almost be Our Lord!"

"—and here are oxen fording a river, men fishing from boats, hunters with their dogs," I continued quickly, displeased.

Fortunately, Mr Bracebridge came to my rescue.

"It is like a magic-lantern glimpse into another world!" he said enthusiastically.

"For which the historian can only be grateful," said Miss Nightingale. "However" – she examined the figures critically – "I must confess that I, not being a historian, am disappointed."

"Disappointed?" I cried. "But why?"

"It is all so extraordinarily literal. Yes, indeed, Mr Wood, here are all the details of everyday life, people working and playing, indoors and out of doors, in sickness and in health, but all portrayed without the slightest hint of composition, without a single one of the touches of art—"

"But, my dear!" expostulated Mrs Bracebridge. "They were at the beginnings of art! You cannot expect from them the things you would look for in the Italians!"

"I would have expected some attempt to reach out beyond the literal," said Miss Nightingale. "That is where everything must start, mustn't it? In the rejection of the everyday, of the merely material. I find nothing of that here. What I find instead," said Miss Nightingale, "is a people trapped in the prosaic."

"Oh, come, my dear!" cried Mr Bracebridge. "You make no allowances! You cannot expect the refinement of a Michelangelo or a Raphael!"

"I am not talking about art," said Miss Nightingale. "I am talking about spirituality. Surely, one would have thought, a people who could construct such wonderful temples, such remarkable tombs, must have had a profound sense of the supernatural? But what do we find? Look at the banal way in which they represent their gods: as creatures with the magnified attributes of animals! This is not the imagination of a priest; this is the imagination of a clerk!"

We began to move through the tall, lotus-budded pillars towards the exit. As we emerged into the sunlight of the portico, Miss Nightingale suddenly stopped.

"What about Trout?"

"Trout?" I cast my eye back quickly over the walls. "I am not sure they are trout. Nile perch, possibly."

"No, no. Trout."

We found her outside, sitting on a stone with her back against a column, knitting. Trapped in the prosaic.

I do not mind admitting that I was feeling vexed as we walked down from the caves. At every turn, it seemed to me, Miss Nightingale was imposing her own conceptions and by doing so was failing to do justice to what was there. Take this question of spirituality, for instance, on which I was certainly no expert. Might it not be that it was there but that she was not seeing it because its representation failed to conform to the conventions she was used to? And was she right, anyway, to dismiss the literal so cavalierly in favour of the ideal? It seemed to me that the argument might cut both ways.

One day, before we left Cairo, I had taken Flaubert and Maxime to visit my artist friend.

His house was one of the old Mameluke ones, with a high outer wall and a succession of courts inside, not unlike a Cambridge college. In the outer court, lying on the grass, we found a camel. Nearby was a tame gazelle, and scattered round were chickens and doves. A covered gallery ran down one side, where one might sit, and behind it rose the walls of the house proper, with its arched, glassless windows filled in with ornate *meshrebiya* lattice-work.

We were led first into the *mandar'ah*, which is a sort of reception room, with a cushioned divan at one end on a dais and a sunken pool paved with coloured marble in the middle, in which a fountain was playing. From there we went into the *mak'ad*, a large hall with a richly decorated ceiling and views of Mecca painted on one wall. The other walls were hung with banners carrying inscriptions from the Koran. There was a divan at one end and another round the great bay window opposite it, from which we could look down into a small secluded garden. A servant showed us to a seat and brought in pipes and a brass chafing dish with hot coals. Flaubert and Maxime accepted and were puffing away on the divan when Jack came in.

I think they at once recognised a kindred spirit. He was wearing a long yellow *galabeah*, red slippers and a white skull-cap embroidered with blue beads. With his closely shaven head and his tuft he looked, I imagine, exactly as they wished to do.

He shuffled off his slippers and climbed up on the divan beside us. A servant brought coffee.

"They would like to see your pictures, Jack," I said after a while.

"You've come just in time," he said. "Tomorrow I am sending them off to England. *The Harem* has been taken for an exhibition."

"*The Harem*?" said Maxime.

"It is what I call it."

He clapped his hands and two servants carried the painting into the room and stood it before us.

"From the life?" enquired Maxime.

"In a way," said Jack.

"Ah!"

We all laughed. I could tell, however, that they liked the painting. Flaubert questioned him closely on his technique. How, for instance, did he allow for the sun? He remarked especially upon the skill with which Jack had treated the fabrics.

"Could you get that," he said, turning to Maxime, "with your photography?"

"I could get the pattern," said Maxime, "but not the colours, of course."

"I am safe for a while yet, then," said Jack, laughing.

"You are safe until eternity, monsieur," said Flaubert, bowing.

Jack merely smiled, but I knew he was pleased by the compliment.

"Let them see *The Meal*, Jack," I said. It was a particular favourite of mine.

The painting was brought in. It shows some men taking their midday meal on a raised balcony, from which they could look down if they wished into a small courtyard with a tree. On the far side of the courtyard there is one of the large box windows that are the glory of the old Mameluke houses. Jack had painted its intricate lattice-work with incredible precision. The strength of the picture generally was in the fidelity with which he had rendered pattern, whether of the rich cushions in the foreground or of the delicate woodwork of the *meshrebiya* screens, and not in the treatment of the figures, which were to my mind rather idealised.

I think Flaubert felt this, too, for after complimenting Jack upon the composition and the colour, he remarked, "Monsieur sees nobility in people's faces."

"I see only what is there," said Jack.

"It is there but it takes the hand of someone like monsieur to reveal it."

He slipped off the divan and went up to the painting to look more closely at how Jack had done the fruit.

"Oh, monsieur," he said, "you are too prodigal. Another artist would have made a still life out of this and thought it enough!"

He passed on to the box window.

"And here the detail is remarkable, too," he said. "Only it is not the same detail. That was the detail of nature; this is the detail of pattern."

"Muslim art is all pattern," I said. "There are seldom humans in their pictures."

"Why is that?"

"I think it is because Muslim tradition reserves the creation of human likeness to God alone."

Flaubert sighed.

"God puts us in our place!" He looked back at Jack's figures and shook his head. "Ah, monsieur, you are not for paradise, I fear. You make too much of us."

He returned to the detail of the window.

"All the same," he said, "there is a kind of equality here. If in this abstraction there is little of man, there is also little of God."

"Unless He is a geometrician," said Maxime.

Flaubert laughed.

Maxime climbed down from the divan, went over to him and looked over his shoulder.

The Dragoman's Story

"I know what you're going to ask me," he said. "You are going to ask me if I could get this with the camera."

"Well, could you?"

"Yes."

"And the nobility, could you get that, too?"

"I get what is there," said Maxime.

Walking down, now, over the hot rock at Beni Hassan, I thought about that exchange. What would the camera see if it were taken to the tomb we had just left? It would record the figures on the wall faithfully, but what would it have to say about their spirituality? Nothing; it would leave that to others. It did not impose its own preconceptions. I felt friendly towards it.

While we were up on the cliffs another boat had passed us. It had set out from Cairo some days after us but, being smaller and faster, had made better progress. It brought with it a bag of mail for the Bracebridges and Miss Nightingale and a letter to me from Aimée.

> Already it seems a long time since you left, and already, no doubt, you are much improved. I begin to question, however, whether the improvement is worth the journey, especially as it means that it is going to take so long . . .
>
> We had your friends round to dinner the other evening and this morning we saw them again after Mass. Maman was much taken by them and ever

since has been talking of a return to France, if only, she says, for the sake of the children. How can a child be French and not know France, she asks? My father looks at me and shrugs his shoulders and I look back and shrug mine, not standing exactly on firm ground in this debate. And, truly, I begin to think I *might* be interested in going back to France, at least for a time, if only to find out what I am missing. Your friends assure me that it is a great deal.

They are an odd couple but I find them interesting, M. Flaubert so quick, M. du Camp so . . . well, I will not say slow, but somehow more solid. This week he has been busy every day with his photographs. He says he would like me to sit for him for a photographic portrait. Maman, I know, would be delighted but I am not so sure. He says that several sittings may be necessary, and I think I know what *that* means! I find French masculinity intriguing; at the same time, I find it hard to take seriously. Perhaps, as Maman says, I have been away from France for too long.

I enclose some pictures that Gérard has drawn. He asks daily after your return. I take his hand and we go to the bank of the river and look up it for your returning boat – so far, alas, without seeing any sign of it . . .

I was not altogether satisfied by this letter. If there was

such a thing as French masculinity, there was also such a thing as French femininity, and Aimée had her share. But while much of the letter was simple teasing, there was enough of substance in it to leave me more than a little disquieted. I did not think there was much real prospect of the family returning to France – Old Bosquet hadn't the money for it – but it was clear that French connections still weighed heavily with Madame Bosquet and in so important and intimate a thing as family relationships they might well prove decisive.

More immediately troubling, however, was the possibility of a liaison developing between Aimée and Maxime. I knew them both well enough to be confident that he had a great deal more experience of such things than she had. He had, too, an attitude towards women that, for all her amused assumption of worldly wisdom, she would not be prepared for. She might be intelligent enough to see through his advances but in such things intelligence is far from being all. That Maxime, and Flaubert, too, for that matter, would lay siege to her, I had no doubt. They would do it as a matter of course. But they would do it only as a matter of course and without any commitment other than to conquest.

What I could have done about it, had I been in Cairo, I was not sure. Madame Bosquet, no doubt, would be only too delighted at what she would see as respectable, even desirable, addresses being paid to her daughter. And what I could do about it now was even more doubtful. I could

101

hardly abandon my duties here, and by the time any letter of mine would reach Cairo, Flaubert and Maxime would probably already have quitted it.

Much troubled, I went up on to the top deck, where, since it was the heat of the afternoon, I would be able to think over my difficulties undisturbed.

Except that almost at once Miss Nightingale appeared.

"Unable to rest, Miss Nightingale?"

"Not this afternoon. It is so hot in the cabin."

"It is even hotter up here."

The sun burned through the awning almost as if it was not there. Heat shimmers danced on the face of the cliff. The woodwork was too hot to touch. Even through the soles of your shoes you were uncomfortably aware of the heat of the deck.

"It will be better in an hour or so."

Miss Nightingale, however, came and sat beside me. She had brought a pile of letters with her. Among them, to my surprise, I could see one from Aimée.

"I asked your fiancée to find out some things for me."

"Oh, really?"

I was a trifle piqued. Surely I was the one who provided information round here?

"Yes. About the position of women in Egypt."

"Ah!"

I did not mind now. This was a field I was content to leave to others.

"What she says is most surprising."

"Indeed?"

"Yes. For instance, apparently the wife retains legal control of her own property even after marriage." She gave me a quick glance. "You will not be unaware, Mr Wood, that such is not yet the position in England."

"No?" And then, as something more definite seemed required, "No."

"There is, of course, growing public interest in the issue."

"I'm sure."

"It is surprising to come out here and to find . . . In a country such as this."

"Well, there you are, Miss Nightingale. One needs to know all sides before coming to a judgement.

"I can understand your feeling that, Mr Wood."

She picked up Aimée's letter. There were more pages to it than I had supposed. Evidently the position of women in Egypt was not something that could be treated with despatch. Certainly not as much despatch as a letter to one's fiancé.

We could see the sandstorm coming for some time before it hit us. The whole southern sky was covered by a dark, swirling, angry cloud. The cloud turned yellow and rolled forward like fog, swallowing up everything in its path. Cliffs, trees, boats, islands, all disappeared. The wind suddenly stiffened and the water became choppy.

The *reis* steered at once into the bank and the crew

rushed to stake the boat heavily fore and aft. Even before they had finished, the *dahabeeyah* began to lurch heavily as the choppiness in the water became waves. The men had thrown some fenders over the side, which was just as well, for the boat began to grind heavily against the bank. On the deck, because of the pitching and tossing, it became hard to stand.

The Bracebridges and Miss Nightingale came up nevertheless.

"One must not miss a thing like this!" said Miss Nightingale.

Already the air was filling with sand. I showed them how to wind cloths round their faces as protection against it.

"It will get into your hair, your eyes, your ears."

The particles were already beginning to sting our faces. On deck the crew was securing everything. They came to me and looked at the awning. I nodded. There was no point in it now anyway. The sun had disappeared and it was rapidly becoming as dark as night. We could see the wind bending the palm trees, and then the opposite bank disappeared.

The wind now had become very hot. It was blowing the sand towards us down the river. The air was so thick with it that you could not tell what was sand and what was water. It was as if the whole river had been blotted out by a monstrous sandbank.

I asked them if they would like to go down.

"One minute more!" said Miss Nightingale.

The *reis* suddenly ran into the cook's cabin and emerged with a loaded gun, which he pointed towards the sky and then fired.

"But why—?"

"To alert oncoming vessels."

Almost at once I saw a boat rushing down on us out of the darkness. It was going so fast that it was past us before I realised that it was upside down.

"They left it too late," I said. "They ought to have tied up sooner."

"But can we not—?"

"No," I said, and hustled them below.

The crew closed the doors, they had previously closed the windows, but it was useless. A thick film of sand already lay over everything, tables, chairs, books, carpet. It thickened even as we watched. A bottle of ink grew a crust around it and then disappeared altogether in a soft bank of sand. In a moment sand had penetrated into every crack, every crevice, into our clothes, into our footwear.

Mrs Bracebridge asked for some water and rather than shout to the steward and run the risk of getting more sand pouring in through the open door, I poured her some from the covered pot we had standing there. Covered it might have been, but the sand had crept into there, too, and the water tasted gritty against our teeth.

"Don't ask for food," I warned. "They will have put the fire out."

Food was, however, probably the last thing they had in mind. Outside, the waves were as big as on the sea, and the *dahabeeyah* was rolling heavily. Mrs Bracebridge complained of feeling queasy and went to lie down. She returned shortly saying that in her cabin the air was so thick with sand that it was hard to breathe. She had only been there for a few minutes but when she had risen from her bed she had left behind her a complete outline of her form in sand.

It *was* hard to breathe. I think that was the worst of it. It always is. I told them to keep their mouths closed behind their cloths and to breathe as slightly as they could. If you opened your mouth at all, even behind the cloth, it seemed to fill in an instant with sand. It was best not to speak.

There was little indeed that one could do. If you opened a book, sand would cover the page before you had time to finish it. It would get in your eyes; even if you closed them it would somehow filter its way in behind your eyelids. I counselled against bathing them until the storm was over. There was sure to be sand in the water and it would only exacerbate the soreness. The only thing to do was to sit there philosophically and endure it.

I could see from my watch that it was night. The Bracebridges and Miss Nightingale returned to their rooms, though not, I fancy, to sleep. I sat on alone in the saloon. Gradually, the heaving of the boat became less and the wind seemed to be blowing less strongly. I wiped the lamp and in the improved light I saw that sand was an inch deep on the floor and covered every-thing.

I loosened the cloth around my face. As I did so, sand fell from the folds. It was still not possible to breathe naturally in the cabin because of the sand suspended in the air.

There is always a time at the end of a sandstorm when you wonder if you would do better out of doors. I sat on a little longer and then went up on deck. There was sand everywhere. It lay in drifts against the cabins, covered the ropes, clogged the crevices in the steering gear. Above, however, I could see stars and knew that the worst was over.

The wind dropped still further and the river quietened. Dawn came and in the light I could see the crew sitting in the *felucca* with blankets round their shoulders, smoking their pipes.

On a sandbank not fifty yards astern of us I could see the remains of the boat that had passed us in the night. Wood, rope and clothes were scattered all over the sandbank and, a little to one side of it, almost covered by the water, was what was left of the hull. It had been a *dahabeeyah* like ours and had, I learned when we put into Manfaloot, been carrying upwards of forty souls.

Mr Bracebridge would have sent a purse ashore for the relief of the families but the *reis* said they would all have come from up river somewhere and would not be known in this area. Before we left, he sent the *felucca* over to the sandbank but that was less, I fear, in the hope of finding survivors than to make sure that there was nothing of value. Later in the morning I saw some clothes hanging out to dry in the *felucca* and one of the men was wearing new slippers.

Seven

A t Osyoot we stopped for twenty-four hours to bake
bread. It was, as I pointed out to Mr Bracebridge,
written into the contract, and besides, it would cause us
no inconvenience as Miss Nightingale wanted anyway to
spend a day here visiting the tombs. They were carved into
the cliffs above the town, which nestled at their foot about
a mile inland from the river, and what was so special about
them, said Miss Nightingale, was that they had served both
as sepulchres, in the time of the pharaohs, and as cells,
later, in Roman times, for the Christian Anchorites of the
Thebaid. There had once been six thousand of them in this
part alone.

"Did you realise that, Mr Wood? This was once a
Christian country."

But first it was necessary to see to the baking of the
bread. As soon as we had tied up at Hamra, which is the
port for Osyoot, the *reis* went off on a donkey to buy grain
and hire an oven. There were large ovens specifically for
the use of sailors, who would go to a local mill and

purchase grain, wash it and grind it on the spot, knead it with their feet and then take it to the ovens for baking overnight. In the morning they would take it out and cut it into slices, which would be allowed to dry in the sun. In this way they made something like ship's biscuit, hard, rusk-like bread which would last them for the next stage of the voyage.

Usually the baking would be done by the sailors themselves, but on this occasion, the *reis* said, it would be done by "Mustafa's womans".

"Mustafa's womans?" said Miss Nightingale.

Mustafa was our cook and he had a wife, indeed several, possibly in every port on the river but certainly at Osyoot, and he agreed to allow Miss Nightingale to visit her. I had warned Miss Nightingale that the accommodation would be humble but, of course, a cook on a *dahabeeyah* such as ours counted as wealthy on the river, and the house, although made of mud brick, was a substantial one, built on two storeys and possessing a yard. The floors were of mud and there was no furniture, but there were slaves.

We were taken upstairs to the main room, where Mustafa's principal wife had spread out a carpet for us to sit on. She was most beautifully dressed in cashmere trousers, a *yelek* of exquisite silk, crimson and white, with gold binding, a *tob* of lilac silk, with immense hanging sleeves, and a long veil of purple gauze, embroidered with silver. Mustafa himself was similarly splendid. Custom required that he display himself and his household to advantage, and I feared that he had borrowed heavily to do so.

Slaves brought sweet, sticky cakes, which Mustafa's second wife took from them at the door and brought to us on the carpet.

"Yes, Miss Nightingale," I said later, "it was an honour. She would not normally do the serving herself. The slaves would do it. But then, he could not afford to dress them as well . . .

"No, Miss Nightingale, distinctions have to be pre- served. There is a difference between first wife and second wife. You will have noticed that the second wife was not so richly dressed . . .

"Well, no, one does not normally see such dress. The finest dress is reserved for inside one's own house. No, it is not aversion from ostentation, it is rather, that the husband does not wish to show off his wife to others for fear . . . Yes, that's right. He naturally prefers to reserve her charms for – No, personal gratification is not, perhaps, quite the – And how does she feel about it? Well, it is hard to ascertain, but—"

"And the second wife? I would have liked to have asked her—"

We had, of course, put questions to them. I had translated Miss Nightingale's words and addressed them, through Mustafa, to the ladies. She had admired their dresses and asked after their children. She had enquired as to the baking and complimented them on the cakes. These

111

were, however, hardly the issues that she had wanted to discuss.

Seeking a way in, she had asked them how they spent their days.

"As women do," the senior wife had replied.

But what that was had not quite emerged.

After a few more similarly unrevealing exchanges, much smiling and a prolonged silence, we had taken our leave. Now, as we walked away, she was questioning me fiercely.

"Four, Miss Nightingale. A man is allowed to have up to four wives. And then, of course, he may have concubines."

"Those slaves?"

"Well, yes, probably."

She considered, and then started again.

"Your fiancée, Mr Wood, says in her letter that the child of a slave wife inherits equally with the child of the real wife?"

"That is so, I understand."

"On the face of it, that is generous. It equates the slave with the free woman."

"Yes."

"But, by the same token, it equates the free woman with the slave. Is not that revealing?"

"Well, yes, I suppose so."

"Does it not say something about the way a woman is viewed in this country?"

"Well, yes, it could be argued—"

"A woman is but a slave. That is all she is and all she can be."

"Well, I don't know that I would—"

"What other possibility is open to her?"

"Well—"

"It was not always thus, Mr Wood. Fifteen hundred years ago there was at least one other vocation open to her if she wished."

"Oh, yes?"

"A life of service in a religious house. But then Egypt was a Christian country!"

Ahead of us I saw the donkeys and escape.

"A widow has quite a degree of independence in this country," I ventured, helping her up into the saddle.

"I would hope it was not necessary to go to those lengths!" said Miss Nightingale.

"Brown, brown, brown!" said Mrs Bracebridge, vexed, her sketchbook open on her lap, her crayons idle beside her.

"Everything is brown," said Miss Nightingale. "The ground is brown, the houses are brown, the people are brown."

"The clothes?" I countered.

She had taken up a position near the landing stage, from which it was possible to see people coming and going on their way to or from the ferry.

113

"When they have any!" said Miss Nightingale. It was true that many of them were scantily clad.

"Even the river is brown. The sand drains everything of colour," complained Mrs Bracebridge, folding up her stool.

If it did, then later the sun gave it back. At sunset the river turned first from brown to copper; then, with incredible speed, other colours appeared, red, blue, green, orange. Not, as Mrs Bracebridge said, the colours of the rainbow, they were too faint, but the colours of metal suddenly cooled, of ore run out of the furnace. She picked up her sketchbook again and this time, her paints.

"Are you not inspired, Mr Wood?" she asked.

"I fear it would beyond me," I confessed.

"It is beyond me, too," said Mrs Bracebridge, "Nevertheless—"

Because she was engrossed, the *reis* went on sailing, long after the sun had dipped behind the palm trees. There were still colours on the water and Mrs Bracebridge was still painting, so he lowered the main sails and let the boat run on under half sails. The wind dropped, as it often did at night, and the heavy *dahabeeyah* could only just make way against the current. It moved so gently that we did not even disturb the water buffaloes standing dreamily in the shallows or the ibises standing reflective on the sandbanks.

The sun disappeared altogether and Mrs Bracebridge reluctantly put down her paints, but the boat still moved on. The Nubian steersman, high up on his platform, seemed to have no difficulty in seeing. He stood there like a great black statue, one hand on the huge tiller, looking intently ahead of him.

The moon came up; and now here was a strange thing. It was not just that it was as light as day, for that one is used to in Egypt. It was that there was still colour everywhere – colour luminous in the oranges that hung in their net from the top of the cook's cabin, colour glowing from the cliffs, colour deepening from the ladies' shawls and the red band which the cook wore round his waist when he went down to lay the places for our evening meal.

Still we continued on our way until at last, some two hours after sunset, the *dahabeeyah* turned in to the bank. The spell, however, remained with us and after dinner we returned to the top deck and sat there looking out at the sandbanks on the other side of the river and the palm trees shining in the moonlight. The crew, too, felt the spell for one of them approached me and asked if they could make some music.

"We have, after all, paid for the instruments," I pointed out.

"Then let us hear them!" cried Mr Bracebridge.

The instruments were, in fact, only two, the *tar*, which is a kind of tambourine, and the *darabukkeh*, which is a funnel-shaped drum held under the left arm and played with the fingers of the right hand. They are, of course, accompanied by voice. There is a principal singer, who

115

gives the lead and, as it were, interrogates the others, and a chorus, which sometimes replies to him and at other times falls in behind him. The pitch is different from ours and the principal singer frequently uses a kind of quavery vibrato which seems strange, indeed, barbaric, to our ears. But then, as Mr Bracebridge said, that fitted our situation, which certainly seemed strange enough, we Europeans sitting up there in our deckchairs with the top deck bright about us, the crew squatting below in the shadows of the foredeck, their turbaned faces turned, rapt, towards the singer, their hands clapping a rhythmic accompaniment, while the quavery notes drifted out across the water.

I do not know how the music struck the Bracebridges and Miss Nightingale – they were rather silent – but to me, more used to it, perhaps, it had its charms. I found myself joining in the clapping; that is, until I caught Miss Nightingale's amused eye. I think, however, she may not have found it too discrepant with our previous mood, for when the performance was over, and the crew had retired to their *felucca*, she did not follow the Bracebridges when they went below, but remained up on the top deck. We sat for some time in silence watching the shadows cast by the palm trees on the water and then she said, "The moon is not like our moon. In England, the moon is always so low in the sky, at least in summer, that you get used to there being enormous shadows. Here, the moon is directly overhead and there is little shadow. When even the moon is different, why should one expect the countries to be the same?"

At Kenna we went ashore to visit our consul. When the Nile is high, you can go right up to the town by water but now the houses were a good mile from the river. To get to them we had to take donkeys and cross a ploughed field and a dried-up tributary of the river where the banks were so steep that the donkey-boys had to hold Miss Nightingale on.

The consul's house was a mud-brick building two storeys high. The top storey had heavily latticed windows and was, presumably, the harem room. We were shown into the lower one, which opened into a yard. Chairs were placed for Mr Bracebridge, Miss Nightingale and myself and a boy was assigned to hold Miss Nightingale's parasol. We were received by the consul's two sons, to whom we gave our letter of introduction from Mr Murray. They pressed it to their foreheads and then sat down upon a hen-coop.

Shortly afterwards, their father appeared. He was a splendid sheikh in, Miss Nightingale calculated, at least four robes (Muslims, she remarked, evidently dress warmly) and three turbans. He kissed the letter and offered us bread and salt. Some turkeys came into the room, which we were invited to feel and, indeed, buy. Miss Nightingale would have liked to have asked if she could meet the sheikh's wives but somehow the opportunity did not present itself. Instead, we handed over our mail and asked him to forward it to Mr Murray.

As we went out, he said, "And will you be wanting dancing girls?"

Kenna was well known for its dancing girls and their numbers had recently been reinforced by those deported from the capital. I asked Flaubert on his and our return whether he had taken advantage of the opportunity to catch up with them. He said, vexed, that he had been so excited by his discovery of the street of the *almeh* at Kenna, and then by finding out that the word *almeh* stands for both prostitute and learned woman ("One would think that they had been in France!") that he had somehow lost sight of the other entertainment that Kenna provided.

It was, of course, at Esna, not at Kenna, that Kuchuk Hanem danced 'the Bee' for him. In the Bee, the performer sheds her clothes as she dances, until she is left with only a tiny square of silk, the size of a lady's pocket handkerchief, which she pretends to hide behind. As a dance, Flaubert preferred the one she had performed for him the previous day, which had involved no divestiture of clothing and had consisted chiefly of a rhythmic leaping in which one foot is brought up alternately in front of the other and then stamped down hard ("African," he said, "in its brutality"). As a dancer, he preferred another *almeh* whom he saw dance at Assouan – Asizeh – who danced, first, the dance in which the neck slides to and fro sideways on the vertebrae ("the effect is as of decapitation") and, secondly, the belly dance, in which the abdomen moves but the face remains expressionless.

It was not, of course, solely the dancing that interested him. He had sexual congress, memorably, with Kuchuk Hanem, with Asizeh, and with many other *almehs*, which accounts for him leaving Egypt with the infection which has afflicted him ever since.

Yet it was not that either, I think, which was in the end his true preoccupation. When he spoke about it afterwards in Cairo, what he lingered on was the rich strangeness of the detail: the large tarboosh that Kuchuk wore, with its gold disk and imitation emerald; the small spray of white artificial flowers pinned to her hair; the blue writing tattooed on her arm; the huge trousers striped with pink, which afterwards she pulled up to her neck; the Abyssinian slave who carried on each arm, like a burn, the round scar of the plague; the room lit by three wicks in glasses full of oil, casting quivering, mysterious shadows; her smell, like that of sweetened turpentine; the music, played by a half-blind man and a child.

All these things besieged his senses. They were what he had come to Egypt for. And they were really there. But, somehow, so great was his romantic hunger, that he bound them all together in one great, exotic, erotic mixture, into a splendid barbarism which he labelled 'African' or 'the Orient' – and which wasn't there at all. He saw so much of Egypt and yet whenever he moved away from the detail this other thing got in the way.

119

*   *   *

"And will you be wanting dancing girls?"

No, I said, we had dancing girls of our own.

The consul looked at Miss Nightingale, puzzled.

I wonder when it begins? Three-year-old Sophie, another
of the Bosquets' brood, used to attend, once each week, a
sort of play party held in the grounds of the Italian Chef de
Mission. Among the children she played with was a little
blond boy, also three years old. Whenever, in recounting
her doings, she happened to mention this little boy, her
hand would fly up to her hair and she would given an
arch toss of her shoulders.

"*Une vraie francaise*," said old Bosquet, laughing.

Aimée and I discussed it, observing that even at so
young an age there seemed to be definite physical pref-
erences.

"It is more marked among girls," said Aimée. "That
is because they grow up faster than boys. They are
playing mothers when the little boys are still throwing
their sticks."

"We were hunting lions," I pointed out. "Is it not rather
that in play children rehearse the roles of adulthood, only
that in the case of boys, the role is no longer what it was?
Women are still mothers but men, which is probably just
as well for me, are no longer hunters."

Among the letters that we collected from the consul
was one for me from Aimée.

Your hunting skills are missed. This afternoon we went for a picnic on Roda Island with your friends. Gérard was expecting support in the chase but M. Flaubert lacks your skill with the spear and M. Du Camp was preoccupied with photographing the palace of Mohammed Bey. Setting up the apparatus took a long time and after a while Gérard wandered off among the carob trees. When papa called him, he would not return. I was sent to fetch him and found him sitting discontentedly on the steps going down to the river. Even the fish, it seems, were resisting his spear. Coming back to the picnic spot, he complained bitterly of your absence. What was the point of a picnic without a hunt? To his complaint I naturally joined my own . . .

It was the things unsaid that troubled me. Aimée's relationship with Maxime and Flaubert had obviously progressed. They were going on picnics together now. And what was the point, as Gérard had said, of a picnic without a hunt?

For days Miss Nightingale had been talking of Thebes. Now, as we approached, she became so excited that she ordered a basket to be brought and climbed up on it in order to see better. The basket contained hens and in the fetching, the catch which fastened it had been dislodged, and once it had been put down, the hens ran out. So there

121

was Miss Nightingale, standing on a wicker basket, hens all about her, impatient to catch her first glimpse of the 'hundred-gated' city of the ancients.

A cliff concealed the Valley of the Tombs of the Kings, but there, on our left, were the famous temples of Luxor and Karnak, and away to the right, above the mud-brick houses, we could see the Ramesseum and the towering figures of the colossi. It was what she had come to Egypt to see and yet at once, I could tell, she was disappointed. More than disappointed: shocked.

"What is it, Miss Nightingale?"

"They have spoiled it," she said.

I looked, and for the life of me I could not see to what she was referring. A sweep of sandy shore. Behind it the houses of the consuls, each with its flag flying. Behind them the mud walls and pigeon towers of the modern village. In front, a host of *cangias*, *feluccas* and *dahabeeyahs*, fishermen with their nets, heaps of tackle of all sorts, some donkeys, two camels whose riders had evidently just come in from the desert and, a little to one side but very close to us, the ancient remains of the temple of Luxor. There were the two great towers of the original gateway, ruined now but still magnificent; before them, two huge black granite heads thrusting up out of the sand; and in front of them, half buried also, a single red obelisk, covered with hieroglyphics. All around were other towers, other heads, colonnades.

"Is it the sand, Miss Nightingale?"

The Dragoman's Story

"No," said Miss Nightingale, "it is not the sand."

And now I saw it, saw what had been there, of course, all the time, but what, being used to it, I had taken for granted and now saw anew through her eyes. Scattered everywhere among the ruins were mud hovels and filthy sheds, foul yards which people and animals appeared to share indiscriminately, squalid little alleyways in which the women knelt grinding their corn while their children played nearby in the mud, their eyes running with yellow matter and the open sores on their faces black with flies. Goats and donkeys grazed beneath the columns and in durra-stalk pens deep with dung, men and animals lay together while black-gowned women walked down to the river with jars balanced on their heads. To me it was ordinary Egyptian village life; to Miss Nightingale it was desecration.

"With such grandeur all about them," she said in anguish, "how could a people sink so low?"

"The Parthenon," said Mrs Bracebridge.

"The Colosseum," said Mr Bracebridge.

"St Peter's, perhaps," amended Mrs Bracebridge.

We were at Karnak. It was only a brief visit since we were reserving our main sightseeing for the return journey but the Bracebridges had been eager to catch at least a glimpse of the famous temple. Glimpse, actually, was all we were getting, for the only time we could fit it in – the wind remaining fair and the *reis* anxious to

123

proceed on his way at dawn the next day – was that evening. We had dined early and set off immediately afterwards. The night was dark and for some time all we could see were the white gowns of the men running beside us to protect us against bandits. But then the moon had come out and we had found ourselves in the middle of a long avenue of gigantic sitting sphinxes, two lines of them, their broken faces turned inwards towards us; which had given us, as Mr Bracebridge remarked, an authentic pharaonic shudder.

The top of the palm trees made black patterns against the moonlight; little black dogs slunk silently along in the sand beside us, waiting for an opportunity to attack, or stood upon the flat tops of the houses barking their hostility.

We had emerged from beneath the palm trees to see the great gate of the Ptolemies ahead of us, passed through it and then, leaving the Temple of Khonsu sleeping on our left, had ridden slowly across the huge square, feasting our eyes on the long skyline of the main temple. Another avenue of sphinxes, ram-headed this time, led up to its entrance. We passed between the towering pylons and came out into the grand court of King Shishak, who captured Jerusalem and carried off the treasures of the Temple of Solomon. The court was as bright as day but without its heat. Around the wall was a line of sphinxes; a hill of stones poured from a fallen pylon. The statues in front of the temple were like gods emerging from the shadows between the columns. In the centre of the court the tall papyrus column shone as white as ivory.

We passed beneath another once mighty pylon, its columns now heaps of shattered stones, and arrived at last in the forest of gigantic pillars which was the famous hypostyle hall. All around us they reached up into the darkness. Only in the middle, where a double row of columns was open to the stars, was there any light, except where the moon shone through occasional gaps in the stone, opening eerie white patches among the shadows.

It was strangely quiet, partly because the temple was now carpeted with sand, which deadened the sound made by our footsteps, but also, I think, because, confronted with such majesty, it was natural to subdue one's voice in respect. The word that comes to me is awe.

I could not but feel that Miss Nightingale's response must surely be very different from her one at Luxor. Here were no incompatible hovels, no jarring people to spoil her communion. Here instead was a grandeur purged of human association, to which she could surely give her assent.

We went back out into the courtyard and stood beneath the ivory papyrus column and looked back at the great building.

"The Parthenon," said Mrs Bracebridge.

"The Colosseum," said Mr Bracebridge.

"St Peter's, perhaps," said Mrs Bracebridge.

Miss Nightingale said nothing.

*   *   *

Hardly surprisingly, I was the only one up early the next morning. Miss Nightingale had fallen asleep on her donkey on the way home and had had to be held on and the others were in little better plight. This morning they were sleeping in. I was awake early, however, partly because it is a trick of my constitution and partly because there was such a commotion on the bank. Hens were clucking, geese cackling, turkeys gobbling. When I looked over the side there seemed to be dozens of them milling about.

Mustafa, our cook, was laying in provisions. He was walking about among the birds, feeling breasts and bargaining with owners. It was a process that we often saw but which had to be done particularly expeditiously this morning as the *reis* was eager to get on his way. The Nubian was already up on the steering platform and the tiller untied. The crew were standing by to help. As soon as Mustafa had made his choice, one of them would pick the bird up and throw it into the *felucca*, where, after some startled squawking, it soon settled down.

The last bird was thrown, Mustafa returned on board and the men cast off. The *dahabeeyah* moved out into the middle of the river and pointed its bows upstream. The hubbub of the shore died away.

The Bracebridges and Miss Nightingale slept on. Mr Bracebridge joined me eventually for a late breakfast and Mrs Bracebridge emerged from her cabin shortly before lunch. Miss Nightingale, however, remained below and I did not see her until just before dinner. She was not very communicative during the meal and afterwards went up on deck alone. When I went up some time later I found her standing by the rail gazing out into the darkness. Not wishing to intrude, I sat down quietly in one of the deck chairs.

"Saint Pachomius," said Miss Nightingale suddenly.

I was not sure whether she was speaking to me or to herself.

"Saint Pachomius," she said again, looking round.

I got up and joined her.

"Saint Pachomius, Miss Nightingale?"

"Do you know who he was, Thomas? He was a Christian saint who lived here in the fourth century. He had a tremendous following – six thousand in the Thebaid generally, over a thousand on the island of Tabenna alone. At that time Egypt was a Christian country; Alexandria was the centre of the Christian world. It was what Rome had been. It was here in Egypt that the great religious debates took place, to Egypt that religious scholars came. Many of the great ideas of Christianity came from Egypt. Did you know that, Thomas? It was here that monasticism started. Egypt is the birthplace of monasteries, it is where all our great holy orders began. Christian, Thomas, Christian! Egypt was Christian. Everywhere it was Christian!"

She was silent for a little while and then started again.

"Everything passes away. That is what Karnak says, isn't it? The pharaohs, the Ptolemies, Greece, Rome.

Christianity, too? Surely it cannot be! Principalities and powers, yes, the rulers of the world. But religion? Christianity? It cannot be. God would not allow it. And yet—"

She was gripping the rail tightly.

"And yet," she said shakily, "when I look round me, what do I see? What remains of Christianity in Egypt today? The Copts? They are despised even by the Muslims. And so often, rightly." She looked at me. "I have not forgotten, Thomas, those dreadful swimming beggars. Is that what Christianity is reduced to here? Is that how a religion ends? In degradation? All religions? The Muslims, too? Is that the explanation of what we saw at Luxor? What is it about this country that seems in the end to degrade everything, to reduce everything?"

"It is very old," I said.

"It is all a matter of time? Yes, that is what Karnak said. But it cannot be right, Thomas, it cannot be right! It cannot be right!" she repeated vehemently, staring out into the darkness.

Eight

They never met. Flaubert's boat did not set out till two months after ours and by the time he had returned to Cairo, the Bracebridges and Miss Nightingale had long departed. His boat made the same journey as ours, of course and, like us, he stopped at Osyoot to allow the crew to make bread. Like Miss Nightingale, too, he climbed up to the old rock tombs, and it was there, 'with an air of mystery' that his guide took him by the hand and showed him the print of a woman's shoe in the sand. The shoe was that of an Englishwoman who had passed that way some time before. I like to think that it was Miss Nightingale that the shoe fitted.

What might they have discussed had they been at Osyoot at the same time and met one evening? Until I returned to Cairo I would have said that they would have found it difficult to converse at all for they had nothing in common, but it was then – on the occasion that Maxime told me about the Englishwoman's footprint – that I learned of Flaubert's astonishing knowledge of the saints of the Thebaid.

It came out during an account of the visit they had paid to a Christian monastery. When their hopes of lodging for the night had been disappointed, they had been taken in by a hospitable Christian farmer, with whom they had spent the evening discussing Saints Anthony and Athanasius. I said that it sounded as if it had been a sparkling evening.

"It was very interesting," said Flaubert, displeased.

Maxime had then taken me aside and warned me that I was touching a sore spot. Flaubert had, it appeared, a particular interest in the subject. Indeed, he had written a novel about Saint Anthony.

"Which I advised him not to publish," said Maxime. "I, and other friends."

This had occurred shortly before their departure for Egypt; and, in Maxime's view, it had coloured the whole expedition. Flaubert, I learned now, had been very depressed throughout, and in particular during their voyage southwards.

"No interest in anything," said Maxime. "He just sat there hour after hour, reading."

I had found this hard to reconcile with the Flaubert I knew, the – almost – model tourist, but Flaubert himself had confirmed it later in the evening.

"I was a bit low at times," he admitted. He then went on to say that the verdict his friends had delivered had come as a heavy blow.

"Perhaps you paid too much attention to it," I suggested.

"No, no," he said. "They were quite right. One should not publish until one is quite sure. Let this be a lesson to you, young Thom-ass," he said to me. By this time he knew of my photographic ambitions. "Do not rush into" – he looked at Maxime – "what do photographers rush into? Print, certainly, but print for the photographer is still a private stage. Exhibition?"

"Exhibition, if you are lucky," said Maxime. "The analogy is more with painting. If you are a photographer, you don't rush anywhere. You just leave your photographs lying carelessly around for people to admire them."

"All the same," said Flaubert, brooding, "it was a heavy blow. It was a verdict not just on the book but on me."

"Nonsense!" Maxime broke in hurriedly.

"It felt like that!" Flaubert insisted. "It cast doubt on my capability of achieving, of ever achieving—"

"Thomas is quite right," said Maxime. "You should not make too much of this."

Flaubert shook his head.

"No, no," he said. "Suppose the judgement is correct? Suppose the talent isn't there?"

"There can be no doubt about that!" declared Maxime.

"Oh, but there is," said Flaubert. "There is! One has to find evidence in oneself before one can be sure. And if one cannot find it?"

He looked at Maxime.

"She is still on at me," he said, referring, I knew, to his mother.

So what might they have talked about had they met? Saint Anthony, of course, and the saints of the Thebaid. Nevertheless, I hold to my view that, given the state of mind they were both in, the subject might not have led to a sparkling evening.

Mrs Bracebridge sniffed.

"But, surely—"

"Yes, madam," I said, "it is castor oil."

She was holding one of the curious girdles that little girls wear south of the Cataract. They are, in fact, the only thing that little girls wear. In some cases they are trimmed with beads and shells but in this case even ornamentation was lacking.

"The garment is immersed, when new, in the oil," I said, "which softens and darkens the leather. It also gives it the curious smell."

The plant grows in abundance south of the Cataract, I explained, and the Nubian makes considerable use of it. From its berries he extracts an oil which he uses for cooking. His sons anoint their bodies with it, his daughters and wives their plaited locks. His garments and blankets are often soaked in it to make them supple. His home and person therefore smell of it.

"It is," I concluded, "the smell of Nubia."

We were at Assuan, the Gateway to Nubia. On the one side the town of Assuan, on the other the island of Elephantine form the pillars of the gates. From them, hills stretch back into the Libyan desert on the one hand and the Arabian desert on the other. On the Libyan side the hills are almost entirely covered with drift-sand, great golden and amber swathes with a sheen like satin. Closer to, the rocks jutting out are of red granite, almost, at times, the colour of plums. On the eastern side, where the rockiness of the hills is more apparent, the red granite boulders at the water's edge have become coated with a glistening skin of black. About four miles further up the river, where the first Cataract begins, the rocks draw in on both sides and you are confronted with the line of rock which divides Egypt from Africa.

It was our last day in Egypt. Tomorrow we would ascend the Cataract, a prospect, I assured them, which was both exhilarating and exciting. Miss Nightingale, I felt, could do with some exhilaration. For the whole of the four days journey between Thebes and Assuan she had remained below in her cabin, suffering, her maid reported, from a headache. The Bracebridges had exchanged glances. It was, I suspected, a recurrence of her old problem.

This evening, though, she had come out and joined us in a tour of the Assuan bazaars.

"The smell of Nubia?" she said, taking the girdle from Mrs Bracebridge and holding it to her nose. "How disconcerting! To me it is the smell of the nursery!" She put the girdle down. "It would be a curio only," she said half-regretfully.

The markets of Assuan are different from those of most of Upper Egypt. Gone were the scarab beads and funerary statuettes of Thebes, gone the little coloured wooden ships of the dead and the pieces of mummy coffins and mummy linen, gone the bright-blue saucers of the tomb. Into their place had come the things of Africa: ostrich plumes, leopard skins, porcupine quills, hippopotamus-hide whips, gold nose rings and ivory bracelets cut direct from the tusk.

We saw the girdles again later, this time being worn. I had taken the Bracebridges and Miss Nightingale down to the camp of the traders, which is one of the great spectacles of Assuan. Here, among huge bales of cotton and of gum arabic, among the sacks of henna leaves and the piles of leopard and lion skins, stalked tribesmen of all sorts: Bishari from Tripoli; Beja, with their fuzzy hair, from the Red Sea hills; dark-skinned merchants from Kordofan and Darfur; bronze Nubians; Abyssinians with almost a tint of blue; as well as traders from even further afield, Guinea, the Yemen, Turkey.

A little to one side, beneath a palm tree, some young girls, the oldest of whom could not have been more than fourteen, were preparing their evening meal. Noticing that they were wearing girdles like the one we had inspected, we stopped for a moment to watch them. Some were kneading dough, others spreading it on what appeared to be pieces of iron plate. The plates had obviously been heated in the fire for after a moment or two other girls peeled the dough off as a flat cake. They were chattering happily as they worked, hardly glancing up at us as we stood there.

A man came up and called one of the girls aside. He took out a stick, measured her height with it and then wrote it down. She went back to her place and he called out another girl.

"Why is he doing that?" asked Mrs Bracebridge, puzzled. "A father, I could understand, but they cannot all be—"

"It affects the price," I said.

"Price?" said Miss Nightingale.

"These girls are slaves. They are on their way to be sold."

They were shocked, I could tell, but did not comment, and I led them quickly away.

At the edge of the camp some boys had spread out various objects on the ground which they were offering for sale. These were humbler goods than we had seen in the bazaar: plaited baskets, some gourds, ostrich feathers and eggs, some brightly coloured birds in wicker cages. Miss Nightingale stopped and bought some ostrich eggs.

"I think I prefer what is natural to Africa," she said, "to what is man-made."

That was the only reference she made to what we had seen. She seemed otherwise to have put it out of her mind, and I was pleased, for I had feared that the sight might have aggravated her indisposition. Instead,

135

with one of those odd mood swings of hers, she seemed almost cheerful as we walked back to the boat.

We had barely reached the top deck when a man hurried up the gangplank behind us leading a small ape by the hand. He had evidently observed us at the camp and followed us. The ape, a young one, was in excellent condition and had been caught very recently in the wild. It had a green head and a yellow throat and upper chest ("Like a bib," said Miss Nightingale) and, despite the recency of its capture, was yet sufficiently tame to lay its paws on the ladies' laps. They pronounced themselves charmed and Miss Nightingale went to fetch it some dates.

"Africa," she said, "has come on board."

And yet we had not yet entered Nubia. That was the business of the following day. We breakfasted early so that the cook could extinguish his fire before we began the ascent of the Cataract. Everything moveable on deck was carried into the cabins to clear space for the men. They were already assembling on the quayside. Two elderly men dressed in white came on board, squatted down on the deck and began talking to the *reis*.

"The sheikhs of the Cataract," I said. "They will take over the captaincy for the passage of the Cataract."

The *reis* got to his feet and came across to me.

"The sheikhs say that the boat is too big to be got up the rapids," I translated for Mr Bracebridge's benefit.

"Oh, that *is* disappointing! Are they sure? We had been so looking forward to—"

"I think they are talking money," I said, "not transportability."

"Oh!"

"Would you permit me?"

I had to settle for rather more than the price we had agreed the day before; but then I had allowed for that anyway.

The Cataract Arabs now filed on board and spread along the deck, perching themselves precariously on their heels on the gunwale. "Like birds," Miss Nightingale said. Our own crewmen were now striking the various structures forward and moving them aft. Kitchen, woodstove, *goullel* were all dismantled and piled against the front of the cabin. The two large boxes and the hen-coop came back to serve as base.

"It will be quite stable, Mrs Bracebridge."

"Stable?"

"We are being asked to stand on it during the passage. We shall be out of the way and it will offer a better vantage point from which to view the proceedings than the top of the cabin."

"The awning?"

"I'm afraid not, Miss Nightingale. Parasols, perhaps?"

As we approached the foot of the Cataract, the river widened out into a huge lake, over half a mile across. Everywhere there were islands: some, mere bundles of rocks, others, yellow with sand, yet others, purple with lupins. The rocks were of different colours, many of them black, but others red and purple, and worn into fantastic shapes, to which our ladies imaginatively ascribed the characters of sea beasts or creatures from legend. On the bigger islands there were trees: palms of various sorts – dom palms with their curious, brown, nut-like husks; date palms with the young dates packed together like compressed green beads; and sunt trees with their feathery tufts and yellow blossom; gum trees and tamarisk, all bound together with brightly coloured creepers.

The party exclaimed repeatedly at the picturesqueness of the scene.

"This," I said, pleased, "is but the hors d'oeuvres."

Ahead of us I could see the Cataract. The banks of the river closed suddenly in. The cliffs advanced, leaving only a narrow gap between them, a slope of rocks and water down which the river rushed terrifyingly. Small islands at the top divided the flow into separate streams which came cascading down toward us, kicking and spitting where they met hidden boulders, until they joined together again at the bottom in a white, seething race.

The boat began to bob as it met the turbulence. One of the sheikhs, now up on the steering platform, started to issue orders to the steersman – a new steersman, I noted, imported especially for the task of navigating the rapids. The boat headed in towards the torrent.

The Arabs, who had been squatting peacefully on the gunwale, suddenly leaped over the side.

The ladies cried out in alarm.

"Good heavens!" said Mr Bracebridge.

"Calm yourselves!"

The Arabs were making for the rocks. The first man to reach them, a huge, finely torsoed Nubian, heaved himself out and jumped up on to a boulder.

A rope shot out from the poop of the *dahabeeyah*. The Nubian caught it, ran along the bank, hitched it round a rock and then sat on the coil.

Arabs now appeared from behind every rock and boulder. Two of them seized the end of the rope and ran back with it to the water's edge. One of the aquatic Arabs took the end in his mouth and swam back out to the *dahabeeyah*. The crew caught it up and arranged themselves immediately in tug-of-war formation on the deck.

Another rope was thrown. It fell among a group of Arabs who caught it and promptly fell flat on their backs.

As the rope tightened, other Arabs ran up and arranged themselves along it.

Both teams braced themselves and looked at the bows of the *dahabeeyah* expectantly.

The other sheikh now appeared at the extreme point of the prow, the skirts of his *galabeah* tucked up under him to reveal grey, woollen drawers. He raised his hand.

The men at the ropes settled. Then, as the hand came down, they began to pull.

139

The *dahabeeyah* moved steadily forward into the turbulence but then came almost to a stop as it met the full force of the current. It hung there poised for a moment at the bottom of the incline.

Then the steersman juggled the great rudder bar and conjured up from somewhere an extra puff of wind, sufficient to lift the vessel forward and start it running.

The men on the bank shuffled backwards, their feet scrabbling on the rock, until the effect of the wind died away and they were able to take up the slack. The rope tightened and they began to pull rhythmically: one-to-three-four-rest, one-two-three-four-rest. The boat began to nudge up the incline.

The crew on deck, pulling to a rock, had helped to give the *dahabeeyah* its crucial initial momentum. Soon, though, the boat was abreast of the rock and their usefulness was over. They dropped the end of the rope into the water and went off to sit in the shade of the cabin, leaving the towing to the teams on the land.

Meanwhile, the Arabs who had swum ashore plunged back into the river and were splashing along beside the *dahabeeyah*. Whenever the pace seemed to slacken – for the trick is to keep the vessel moving – or when extra force was needed to bring the boat up over a ledge, they hurled their weight behind it. When an obstacle loomed ahead they rushed forward and threw themselves between hull and hazard, wrestling the boat past by sheer physical effort.

Astonishingly, in this way, the heavy boat moved slowly up the incline.

But this, as Miss Nightingale said afterwards, was not the half of it. It leaves out, for a start, the noise. We suddenly became aware that we were sharing the spectacle with others. Hundreds of Arabs, it seemed, had appeared from nowhere and were racing along the bank abreast of the boat, urging on the tug-of-war teams and shouting excitedly to the men in the water. They shouted back, and to and at each other, and the cries of them all echoed against and were magnified by the cliffs. The din was tremendous.

So was the excitement. Every pull of the ascent seemed to generate its own crisis. Boulders suddenly appeared, men as suddenly disappeared (although they always seemed to flounder up again smiling). Sometimes a stray impulse of wind would catch the sail and send the boat in a direction different from that which was intended, and then the steersman would have to bring it back sharply. Sometimes, too, he would try to coax the boat to 'jump' up from one pool to another, a trick easier to perform with a boat smaller than ours but one which was an important help to the men towing. Sometimes when he attempted this the boat would hang for a moment on an edge and there would be cries of alarm from the bank; but then the swimmers would throw themselves behind it and enthusiastic helpers would jump in from the bank, not always wisely, and the crisis would be resolved.

141

So, incident by incident, crisis by crisis, accompanied by much din and drama, we moved up the incline until at last, near the top, a favourable puff of wind sent the *dahabeeyah* gliding past the remaining rocks and past the tug-of-war teams and the swimmers and out into a calm, blue pool, where it rested, swaying gently.

"In such labours," mused Miss Nightingale, "the humble Arab is quite transformed. Where before he seemed mean and sensual, now he seems almost noble. Where before, God's creation seemed marred, he is now a thing of beauty."

"Yes, indeed," said Mrs Bracebridge, observing, with a painter's eye perhaps, the finely torsoed Nubian, who was sitting now upon a rock, "a positive Apollo Belvedere."

Miss Nightingale frowned.

"I did not quite mean that."

"I know what you mean," said Mr Bracebridge. "You mean that, pitted, as here, against the elements, he takes on titanic proportions."

"We see him in his element, certainly," said Miss Nightingale.

"You see him as he is," I said.

Miss Nightingale turned to me.

"No," she said, "not as he is, but as he might be."

The swimmers were now coming back on board, and we saw how much the struggle had taken out of them. They seemed drained. As each man came on board, trembling, his mouth chattering from the cold, he was wrapped up in a blanket and led forward to where a large brazier was standing in the bows.

"Mr Wood," said Mr Bracebridge, "they have worked hard for us. Do you think a cup of brandy would come amiss?"

"I think it would be greatly appreciated."

There were seven rapids to the first Cataract. The next three were short and straight, like the first, and approached in much the same way. Each took about three quarters of an hour to climb. The fifth rapid, however, was different. The river narrowed sharply and the rocks rose steeply on both sides in a series of ledges down which the water tumbled in sudden falls, leaving shallow pools through which the men on the ropes had to splash. This time, too, the channel wound back in a succession of bends so that the angle of pull was for ever altering.

Ropes were thrown out this time on both sides and long lines of Arabs assembled on each bank. The teams had to pull in parallel and the sheikh went up into the very tip of the bows to supervise things closely. It was only too easy, with the channel always bending, for one team to get out of alignment with the other. Then one rope would suddenly slacken and the other rope take all the strain and the boat swing wildly across the channel. The swimmers would throw themselves en masse between the boat and the opposite bank. The sheikh would gesticulate ferociously – in the roar of water and the general shouting an individual voice could not be heard – and the offending hauliers struggle desperately to recover.

Progress this time was much slower. The current rushed down the pass with such force that it was hard even with additional ropes and extra men to make headway against it. The narrow passage left, too, a dangerously small margin for error. Almost as soon as the *dahabeeyah* began to veer, the swimmers had to hurl themselves into corrective action.

With the hazards so frequent, the drama gained in intensity. It was unsurprising, therefore, that many should come to view it. The cliffs were crowded with spectators. Not just the white-gowned Cataract Arabs themselves but wilder men from the desert, fuzzy-haired and carrying spears and clubs.

Suddenly there was a sharp crack and something whipped across the water. I felt the boat begin to swing even as I realised what had happened. The left-hand rope had parted.

The men on the right bank were struggling to hold the boat on the single rope. They had fallen on to their backs and were trying to wedge their feet against the boulders. Slowly, though, the whole line was slithering forward. There was a heavy bump as the *dahabeeyah* hit the bank. It began to swing out again, met the force of the current and crashed once more into the side. This time it stuck.

Or, at least, the stern stuck. The bows started to swing out but they were held by the rope.

On the deck the crew was rushing to the side with fenders. Both the sheikhs were shouting orders. Another rope snaked out from the *dahabeeyah*. It was caught by some of the onlookers, who immediately belayed it round a rock and clung on tight. The bank was crowded with Arabs now. Another rope was flung out. The *dahabeeyah* steadied.

Then nothing seemed to happen for quite some time.

I jumped down, went to the side and looked over. All along the boat, between the hull and the rocks, was a line of men. For a moment, a terrible moment, I had the sickening thought that they were all pinned there.

Then, one by one, they began to turn round in the water so that their shoulders were placed against the hull, their feet against the rocks. Other men jumped in to fill the occasional spaces. Soon there was a long, continuous, living buffer.

At the rear of the vessel was a little knot of activity. The *reis* was there, peering down into the water and gesturing with his hands. The steersman had let go of the rudder bar and was sitting peacefully to one side.

I walked aft. The Arabs were diving into the river. They remained there for a moment wrestling with something. Then they rose spluttering to the surface and clung to the rocks to recover.

The blade of the rudder had been caught in the rocks.

The men were struggling to prise it free. I could see a little group bent over beneath the surface. One of them shot to the top and said something to the onlookers on the bank. Without hesitation a dozen of them plunged into the water and began to push against the stern of the *dahabeeyah*.

The big vessel moved and a cry of triumph went up from those nearby. It began to move more strongly and I realised that the ropes were taking the strain. The men began to scramble out.

I felt someone beside me. It was Miss Nightingale. She was looking down into the water and her eyes were shining.

"These men are heroic," she said.

The last two rapids were relatively straightforward; in fact, so straightforward that by the time we had reached the seventh one Mr Bracebridge had become a little bored. He got off the boat and made a detour inland, taking his gun with him in the hope that he might find some shooting, and promising to meet up with us behind the last rapids. He invited Miss Nightingale to go with him but Miss Nightingale, hitherto the staunchest and readiest of walkers, insisted on remaining on board.

"I wouldn't have missed this for anything!" she confided to me. "It is one of the most striking things I have ever witnessed."

I was pleased, firstly because I felt that I had succeeded in presenting them with a spectacle worthy of the tour, but secondly because it seemed to have put Miss Nightingale in a much happier frame of mind.

As soon as we had passed the Cataract we climbed down from our vantage point and the crew began to restore the vessel to its normal condition. The awning on the top deck was re-erected and our comfortable chairs re-produced. Mrs Bracebridge settled herself down with her drawing pad and invited Miss Nightingale to join her.

Miss Nightingale, however, preferred to pace about the main deck. Her mind was still dwelling excitedly on the passage of the Cataract.

"It is one of the most striking things I have ever witnessed!" she repeated.

After several vain attempts to persuade her up to the top deck, Mrs Bracebridge abandoned her efforts and took up her drawing pad. From time to time, however, she shot concerned glances at Miss Nightingale.

We were now on a particularly placid stretch of the Nile. Lupin fields came down to the river on both sides. At the water's edge water wheels creaked noisily and yet somehow comfortingly. Small children and wild fowl paddled in the shallows. Further inland the roofs of houses could be seen among the palm trees and, now that it was getting towards evening, the curl of smoke.

The *reis* very soon took the *dahabeeyah* in to the bank and tied up for the night. Mr Bracebridge appeared on the bank with a brace of pigeons. And eventually

Miss Nightingale was persuaded to go below and dress for dinner.

After dinner, though, she came up again on deck. Her excitement had subsided and she was content to stand up on the top deck, leaning against the rail, and looking out over the river luminous in the moonlight, the fields of barley still glowing golden in the half darkness, and the distant silvery palm trees.

The Bracebridges, seeing that she was content, and calm now, went below. I remained on the top deck, on the other side from Miss Nightingale, sharing the peace of the evening.

"There is nothing wrong with God's world," said Miss Nightingale, "really. He knows what He is doing."

She half turned towards me as she spoke and I took that as an invitation to join her by the rail.

"I have never been so excited in my life," she said, a third time. "It shakes one free. In England the outward excitement is small, it is the inner excitement that is great. Here it is the outward call that is great, one feels a kind of instinctive response to the elements and to the elemental. Yes," she said, softly, to herself, "it is the elemental that I have felt today. And it releases, it gives one a sense of power which one has not felt before."

To my surprise I felt her leaning against me. I put my arm around her. I became aware of the pressure of her breast against my hand. She was wearing, in the heat, only a thin dress with little beneath, and I could have sworn I felt her nipple stirring under my palm.

"No, Thomas," she said, disengaging herself and making for the companion way. Again, though, I could have sworn she was smiling.

Nine

I t was with some embarrassment that I met Miss Nightingale next morning at breakfast. She greeted me as calmly and pleasantly, however, as if nothing had happened and, I realised later, skilfully contrived to place a distance between us. As soon as I could, I escaped up on deck and busied myself posing useless questions to the crew and having an unnecessarily protracted conversation with the *reis*, who had now, of course, with the departure of the sheikhs, resumed command of the vessel.

Later in the morning Miss Nightingale joined Mrs Bracebridge up on the top deck, sketch pad in hand. They had been assured (Miss Martineau again?) that the landscape immediately above the Cataract was among the most picturesque in the world. Unfortunately for their purpose, there was a favourable wind and the *reis*, eager to make the most of it, was reluctant to stop at Philae, claiming that we could see it better on the return journey. We therefore passed the island – the Holy Island, as Miss Nightingale insisted on calling it – without going ashore; and ruined temples, romantic, deserted colonnades and mysterious pylons had to remain for the moment uncaptured. The sketch pads were put away unused, for the landscape which succeeded was unremarkable, and the ladies and Mr Bracebridge took instead to their books.

After some hesitation I went up and joined them. Mrs Bracebridge greeted me with a smile from beneath her eyeshade, Miss Nightingale and Mr Bracebridge with pleasant nods. I settled myself down in one of the vacant seats. What else I had expected, I do not know.

We stayed up there until it was time for luncheon and then descended together. Afterward, the others took their siesta. I returned to the top deck and sat there alone, watching the banks go by. I did not see much of them, however. My mind was in turmoil, wondering how best to proceed. Had I overstepped the mark? Should I find some way of offering Miss Nightingale my apologies? But the initiative, as I saw it, had come from her. Were such apologies *de trop*? Might they even be resented? Did she wish me to build on the overture, whichever of us it had come from? Or was the whole thing best forgotten?

Late in the afternoon they came up again, together, and we took tea. We sat for a time chatting idly and studying the banks. There was little there of interest, however. Whereas in Egypt the strip of cultivation on either side of the river had been so wide that one had sometimes forgotten that it was just a strip and that beyond it lay the desert, here, in Nubia, the desert came right in on one side and stony hills on the other. The strip of cultivation was reduced to a few yards. There was room only for a narrow ribbon of date palms and little patches of barley or durra planted out at the water's edge. After a while the others returned to their books.

Gradually the strength went out of the sun. Shadows crept across the river. The Bracebridges closed their books and went below. I waited, with some apprehension, to see what Miss Nightingale would do. She read on for some minutes, then put her book aside, gave me a polite nod and went down to her cabin.

The river in this part of its course wound away in a succession of reaches between banks relieved only by occasional patches of lupin and isolated palm trees. The few villages that we saw were very poor. The huts were mean, the domestic animals thin. The people were desperate to barter but all they could bring to the exchange were pigeons, marrows and strange chameleons which they offered as pets.

At one particularly mean village Miss Nightingale, taking pity, purchased three chameleons, which she kept in her cabin, where they spent most of their time, she reported, hanging themselves up by their tails pretending to be dead in order to lure the flies; surely a redundant exercise, Mrs Bracebridge observed tartly, given their existing over-abundance in the *dahabeeyah*. Might not the chameleons, however, contribute to reducing that abundance? It all came down to range, said Mr Bracebridge, the hunter among us. Even the most expert of the chameleons could project its tongue only some three inches. In an attempt to redress that disadvantage Miss Nightingale fetched a sprig of mimosa and sprinkled it with sugar, bringing about a great concentration of flies, extreme excitement in the chameleons and, shortly afterwards, what Mr Bracebridge described as a veritable Massacre of the Innocents.

At times in that first day or two I even contemplated the possibility of being dismissed. Never having been employed by others before, that was a new experience for me and I did not like it. Hitherto I had not been at all conscious of that side of our relationship. Miss Nightingale and the Bracebridges had always treated me as an equal, as one of the party, and I had come to look upon myself as such, as a gentleman in my own right. What this incident brought home to me, however, was that I was not an equal. I was not even, strictly speaking, a gentleman; at least, not in terms that would have applied in England. My family had been, at best, yeomen and I was really just a poor boy with no prospects who had come out to Egypt to make his fortune. The social distance between us came home to me one day when Mr Bracebridge happened to mention some of Miss Nightingale's connections. It was clear that she was entirely beyond the reach of one such as myself. I told myself that I had been foolish even to entertain the possibility that she had wished things to go further. I had forgotten myself. I had lost sight of my true position.

For this I was inclined to blame my role as dragoman. The fact is that when one is guide to a party, the normal relationship of superiority and inferiority is seemingly reversed. In your care for the party and in your consciousness of their need for you, you tend to think of yourself as the shepherd and of them as the sheep; forgetting that, in this case, it is the sheep that own the shepherd.

Just before Korosko a *cangia* overtook us and made signals. When we reached the village we found it tied up to the bank. It had mail for us, a whole sackful, which after Korosko we settled down to read. In my case that did not take long, for there was only one letter for me, from Aimée.

> Maxime has asked me to pose for him in oriental costume. I am not unwilling, but what does he mean by oriental costume? I think of it as *tob, burko* and *habarah*, which between them cover me entirely, leaving no centimetre of me exposed. He thinks of trousers and a short vest which leaves plenty of me exposed! Where does he get his ideas of oriental dress from? La Triestine?
>
> There is a difference, I tell him, between harem

wear and what one wears when one goes out of the house. It is harem wear that he is thinking of – but, then, I suspect, harem is what he is often thinking of. I put this to him. Just so, he replies, and it is exactly this image which he wishes to capture in his photograph.

In principle, I have no objection to posing, nor even to showing a few centimetres of bare flesh. In practice, I shrink from baring my tummy because to do so would reveal a small blemish which I have hitherto concealed. Do not alarm yourself; it is very tiny. All will, no doubt, one day be revealed to you . . .

To move from high questions of one art to high questions of another: would you, with your next letter, please include a drawing of a crocodile? Gérard asks for that particularly. He was much taken with the sketch of the *dahabeeyah* that you sent us – indeed, it is pinned up on the nursery wall. *Dahabeeyahs*, however, are things he sees every day and lack the force of novelty. But a crocodile, now! And would you please make it green (a touch of crayon, perhaps?) and represent it with its jaws open? This will be nothing, I know, to an artist such as you, but it will give great pleasure (and is not that what art should seek to do?). I add only, on my own behalf, the earnest request that, in your zeal to make as faithful a rendering as possible, you do

155

not approach the living model too closely, especially from the front end. Art, no doubt, should have its price, but some prices would be too much.

Now that we were south of the Cataract we were, in fact, beginning to see crocodiles regularly. They lay on sandbanks, not so much like logs – there was little wood in the river or, indeed, in the whole of Nubia – but, rather, with their yellow and green, blending into the sand and reeds. Mr Bracebridge was anxious to try his gun, but the ladies pleaded that at such close quarters the noise would be unendurable and suggested he wait until we had tied up for the night and he could do his hunting from the bank. The *reis*, in any case, did not wish for the distraction. This stretch of the river, between Korosko and Derr, was full of sandbanks and it was easy to run aground, and while the Cataract Arabs might not mind plunging over the side to assist our passage, it was a different thing this far up the river, where crocodiles abounded. We confined ourselves, therefore, to sketching the crocodiles, not shooting them.

"The touch of pink?" queried Mrs Bracebridge, when I showed her my attempt.

I had to admit that I had improved on nature by giving a sanguinary suggestion to the inside of the creature's throat.

"It will go down well with my patron," I said.

*　　*　　*

The moment of intimacy on the top deck had not been repeated. Miss Nightingale saw to it that we were seldom alone together. Perhaps it was better so.

Each day now it was becoming hotter. When we went for a walk, it could be only in the very early morning or in the cool of the evening. Between these times we kept beneath the awning: except that even there, at midday, it was so hot that soon the others were driven below to the cooler darkness of their cabins.

There was in any case little on the banks to study on this stretch of the river. The ruins were few and usually some distance inland and the heat and the general stoniness of the desert did not incline us to seek them out.

On the Libyan side the stone was sometimes relieved by great gashes of sand which fell in golden drifts from what was often a high rocky plateau. The sand was so smooth, so unsullied, that once we were provoked to attempt an ascent. We soon abandoned it. Our feet sank into the warm, loose sand making funnel-shaped holes which filled again almost at once, almost before we had taken our feet out of them, pulling us back and making it possible to progress only by a kind of upwards flounder.

"It was," said Mrs Bracebridge afterwards, "like trying to walk through deep snow."

At the bottom of the drift she had stopped for a moment looking back up at the great bank of sand, at the sweeps and curves and curls that were for ever altering, for ever forming new shapes, under the continual influence of the wind, and at the subtle, perpetual play of light and shadow across its surfaces. Then she had stopped and had picked up a handful of sand. The individual grains, close to, were silverish, burnished almost to glass by wind and abrasion. By what strange alchemy, she asked, could what was silver be transformed into what was gold?

She had sent for her paintbox, stool and easel and settled herself down in front of the drift. After a moment she had said, "It's not really gold, though, is it? It's amber and apricot, buff and maize, orange."

I was pleased, because once she had seen it all as brown.

Sand is, of course, a basic feature of the country and when you have been here for as long as I have, you take it for granted. You no longer notice the sand in your slipper every morning, the slight, perpetual taste of grit in the food, the irritation of the particles behind your eyelids every time you come back from a walk. But newcomers to the country see it with fresh eyes and different individuals see it differently. Mrs Bracebridge was seeing it with the eye of the artist. Her husband saw it with the more prosaic eye of the man of affairs or, perhaps, the amateur geographer. The sand, he said, was taking over the country. He pointed to the increasing number of sandbanks in the river and spoke of the general encroachment of the desert. Would there come a time, he wondered, when there would be no Nile and the only indication that there had once been a river in these parts would be a gigantic furrow in the ground? We went for a ride inland one day near the ancient port of Mahatta and found the great, dried-up valley where once, five thousand years ago, the Nile had flowed. Would it be thus again?

And Miss Nightingale, I asked myself, how did she see it? What did she see, contained in a grain of sand?

Delayed by the sandbanks, we did not reach Abu Simbel until the evening of the sixth day after ascending the Cataract. The sun had just set and beneath the shadows the water was still fire and bronze. For over two hours now we had been seeing the cliff ahead of us and for the past hour had been able to make out that the front of it was in some way sculpted. Gradually a gigantic facade was revealed to us and, enclosed by the facade, four colossal figures. The figures were carved out of the rock but, sand-coloured, they seemed less man-made than an emanation from out of the sand itself, a strange coming together of the countless grains whose subtle receptivity to form and colour had so struck Mrs Bracebridge earlier.

In those days, of course, the sand had not been cleared away and it came right up to the chin of the northern-most colossus. I believe it was this colossus that, a few weeks later, Flaubert tried to free from the sand, at least its upper part, so that Maxime could get a photograph of the complete head. What Miss Nightingale found was a bank of sand lying right up against the front of the main temple and coming to within three feet of the top of the doorway. To get in she had to crawl through on all fours and then slide down a twenty-foot slope of sand on the other side. At the bottom of the slope all was darkness. The temple was built inside the cliff and the only light and air was that which came from the entrance. It was like dropping into a hole in the ground.

"It was as if," Flaubert told me later, "I had been thrown into an oubliette." One of those pits in which the French used to incarcerate their prisoners.

Mrs Bracebridge was another who found the experience disquieting. She had shrunk back at the entrance and then descended most unwillingly. Inside she was almost overcome by an acute sense of the weight of the mass of rock above. Neither on that occasion nor on later ones could she bear to stay there long.

I had wondered how Miss Nightingale might respond. Positively, it seemed.

At the bottom of the slope she rose from the sand, dusted herself off, and looked round her with curiosity. She found herself in a great hall. As her eyes grew accustomed to the light she was able to distinguish eight colossal figures, four on one side, four on the other, the crook and flail of majesty in their arms, their huge shoulders appearing to support the whole weight of the mountain above.

We sent back for candles and by their light were able to make out that the walls were covered with marvellous reliefs. On later occasions we returned and pored over them but on this first visit were content to secure merely a general impression. Off the main hall were other chambers. We passed through them and came to a small chamber hewn out of the rock, in which there was an altar and behind it four strange figures.

"This is the sanctuary, Thomas, the holiest part of the temple. And these are personifications of attributes of the eternal mind: Ptah, the creator; Ra, the sustainer; Amun-Ra, the hidden mover; and Neph, intellect. There is a kind of progression, you see. In the outer chamber, the great hall, we meet Osiris – those huge figures, they're Osiris – who is the personification of overall goodness, and then here we come to aspects of that goodness, the qualities that make it up. It is an extraordinarily sophisticated conception." She broke off. "But that's not it, is it?" she said. "That's our foolish chatter about them, not what they have to say to us."

She stood there for a long time. I touched her arm but she showed no inclination to move.

The candle I was holding began to die down.

"Miss Nightingale—"

"Yes, we ought to go." At the door, however, she turned and looked back. "I find it incredibly moving, Thomas, to see them still sitting there. Still, after three thousand years. Time means nothing to them, it just washes about their feet. And perhaps that is why they still have something to say to us. Everywhere else in Egypt, Thomas, time has worked to corrupt. It has worked to pull down, to undermine. Where are the saints of the Thebaid now? That is the question that Karnak taunts us with, isn't it? But these four stand outside time. What they said once they say still."

We climbed up the slope at the far end of the hall and crawled out into the sunlight. Below us, tied up to the bank, was the *dahabeeyah* and on its top deck we could see the others, who had long since abandoned us. They stood up when they saw us and waved, and Mr Bracebridge pointed to a tray of cold drinks. Miss Nightingale waved back enthusiastically.

Over the next few days we returned to the sanctuary time and time again. It seemed to hold some special meaning for her, to contain some riddle which she was anxious to tease out.

"They speak to us, Thomas, perhaps they speak to us especially, we modern, over-excited, restless Europeans. They tell us of the possibility of calm. It is the calm of perfect spiritual fulfilment, when everything else has fallen away, all the silly thoughts, the vain distractions, all the – the irrelevant things. We have to put them all away. Everything."

"It was as if I had been put away," said Flaubert. "I looked up at that little round of light and panicked. Out there was sun and life, in here was – I looked up at that little hole and it seemed to be getting smaller and smaller all the time, and I thought it was going to close and that I would be cut off, that there would be no light and no air, I was desperate for air—

"And still am," he added.

She and I were both early risers but on the last morning I had hardly cleared my bedroll away when she appeared on deck. She had wanted, she said, to watch the sun rise and perhaps catch the first rays as they fell on the colossi opposite. I put down the gangplank for her and we both went ashore. Although the air was still quite chilly, the sand was warm and when we sat down, she took off her shoes and buried her feet in it. The top of the cliff went gold and then, as we looked, the light began to creep down. It touched the head of one of the colossi and then lit up its face. By its side, for a moment, the other faces were grey and cold but then they lit up, too. The sun moved on down the cliff and then began to spread across the sand towards us. Suddenly I felt it warm on my back.

Behind us, in the *felucca*, the crew began to stir. Miss Nightingale got to her feet and walked forwards towards the cliff.

"I don't want people," she said.

She stood for a moment looking upwards.

"And yet," she said, "my heart is still with that secret

four, buried away in perfect peace, where no sound ever comes, where no light ever reaches."

These days, of course, the sand has been cleared away. On certain mornings something remarkable happens. As the sun rises above the eastern cliffs, a long ray falls down into the doorway of the temple. It pushes on through the great hall, past the Osiris, still standing there, and on into the sanctuary itself, where it falls upon the altar. I wonder, if she had known that, whether it would have made any difference?

There are, of course, two temples at Abu Simbel and on the third day we went to the smaller one. It was dedicated to Rameses and his queen, Nefertari and, like the other temple, was basically a huge cave carved in the rock, with a massive facade at the front. As with the larger temple, the facade enclosed gigantic figures, only this time there were six of them, three of Rameses and three of Nefertari, each about thirty feet high. Endearingly, they had their children by their side, little ten foot high figures, the sons beside him, the daughters beside her.

"Now here's a thing!" said Miss Nightingale, astonished.

She was looking at the reliefs inside the temple of Rameses and his queens. For now there appeared to be two of them, one a somewhat pug-nosed lady, the other, Nefertari, the principal one, remarkably beautiful still to us today. Neither the number nor the beauty, though, were what had struck Miss Nightingale.

"No, Thomas, it is the *position* that they occupy. They are given as conspicuous a position as Rameses himself! Do you know what that means, Thomas? It means that they are seen as equal to him. And that is extraordinary! It means that three thousand years ago, a thousand years before the birth of Our Lord, man was capable of according woman the position that Christianity gives her today!"

We stopped, in the sanctuary, in front of a broken statue of a cow-headed woman.

"This is Hathor, Thomas, the divine mother. In the place of honour. Honour, Thomas! Not at all how woman is viewed in Egypt now! But that is how Rameses saw his queen. He wished to honour her. That is the point of the whole temple. Come and see!"

She led me outside and, guide book in hand, translated for my benefit the inscription on one of the buttresses.

"'Rameses, the Strong in Truth, the Beloved of Amen, made this divine abode for his royal wife, Nefertari, whom he loves.' Whom he loves, Thomas," she repeated with emphasis. "He offered it to her in love and honour. And she felt the same about him."

She took me back inside.

"It should be about here. Can you bring the candle closer, Thomas? Yes, there it is." She consulted Wilkinson once more. "'His royal wife, who loves him, constructed for him this Abode in the Mountain of Pure Waters.' It was mutual, you see. She built it for him and he built it for her. Because they loved each other and wanted to honour each other. Love and honour. The two go together. As in Christian marriage."

She was speaking theoretically, I think.

"And do you see, Thomas, it was *because* their relationship was like that that he was able to see her as an equal. That is what raises woman. That is what Christian marriage does. And the astonishing thing, the miracle – well, isn't that the right word? I truly begin to think there must have been divine intervention here – is that a thousand years before Christ was born there could have been this – this anticipation of it!"

I had thought she might be addressing me. But she wasn't. She was excited, but only by the idea.

I went back outside. I wanted to look at the ten foot high children again. But the bank cut away sharply at that point and I couldn't get far enough back to see them properly.

Ten

A bu Simbel was the furthest point of our journey south. After spending a few days there we turned and began to come back down the river. Now we had the current with us and progress was easy. There was seldom any need to track; only when the wind blew exceptionally strongly against us, and then we usually preferred to tie up to the bank and wait for it to blow itself out. We could afford to do that for on this return journey our intention was not to hurry but to linger and to look.

When we had passed Philae before we had not been able to go ashore but now we stayed there for several days. Miss Nightingale had been looking forward to this eagerly. She made much of the belief that the island was holy. Tradition held that it was the burial place of Osiris and that in the waters round about it no fish could swim nor, in the air above, birds fly. She hoped that some of its holy peace would pass into herself and as soon as she could she went off alone to reflect quietly in its long, deserted colonnades.

I, too, was glad of the opportunity to step aside from the business of the voyage and engage in a little private reflection. For I was no longer certain of how things stood between myself and Miss Nightingale.

You may feel that no such doubt should have arisen since she had made clear her wishes and allowed the pattern of our relationship previous to the incident to reassert itself. That is so, and if things had rested like that all would have been well. But there were also moments, and not a few of them, when she seemed eager to go beyond that pattern: moments of sudden warmth; solicitations for company; turnings towards me in the party particularly, a new – or so it seemed to me – assumption of intimacy. It was not now, however, intimacy in any physical sense but intimacy in some other sense. I was almost going to say a shared feeling of complicity.

Well, that, you may say, is understandable. We had both been party to an act, or situation, and she was merely recognising that, and generously. Yet I felt that it went beyond that. She seemed often, as I have said, to be taking the initiative. And yet when I responded she at once swiftly withdrew.

I know what you are going to say: that she was being playful. Or that, having indicated a willingness, natural modesty prevented her from going further and that what she really wanted was for me to press her. Well, of course, such thoughts did occur to me too, and I tried to respond appropriately. But when I did, she withdrew in so marked a fashion that I could not but conclude that I had misconstrued her entirely; that that was not what she wanted. What she *did* want, however was by no means clear to me.

One day, nearly our last on the island, Miss Nightingale lingered so long in her colonnade that I feared she would be late for dinner and went to fetch her. I found her sitting on a broken column gazing out over ruins half-submerged among the palm trees and in particular at one great pylon whose top was already tinged with red from the setting sun. She looked up at me and smiled.

"I know what you have come for, Thomas," she said cheerfully. "You have come to fetch me back to life."

She stood up and gave me her arm and we began to walk back through the palm trees to the spot on the bank where the *dahabeeyah* was moored.

"As you always do."

She gave me a surprisingly merry glance.

"Did you know that, Thomas? As you always do. I look upon you as the keeper of my conscience. Or, rather," she went on playfully, "of what I think of as my reverse conscience. In others the role of conscience is to remind them that there is something other than the mundane and the material. In my case I need to be reminded of the importance of that world. I would desert the visible only too readily. What you remind

169

me of, continuously, is that there is a life here which our Lord thought so important that he came down to join it."

Which did not make things any clearer.

According to Maxime, much later, back in Cairo, Flaubert, who had been bored throughout their journey, had reached a particular peak of boredom during the days they had spent at Philae, where he had passed most of his time sitting in a colonnade reading. This had exasperated Maxime, who complained that Flaubert had not made the most of the opportunities offered him by the voyage. He had been too content, said Maxime, just to sit up there on the top deck of the *dahabeeyah* and let the world pass before him, "Like the screen of a panorama mechanically unwinding."

'Panorama'? I was not sure at that time what exactly that was. Maxime told me that the panorama had been all the rage in Paris just before their departure. It was, said Maxime, essentially a sequence of pictures moved past a point so as to give a viewer at that point the illusion of succession in time, of a scene gradually advancing and changing. A moving picture, so to speak.

Panoramas had probably come into his mind because while they were staying at Thebes they had met the celebrated Colonel Langlois, there to make sketches for a panorama he intended to produce on the ruins of Karnak. He had, said Maxime, previously created a very successful one on the theme of 'The Battle of the Pyramids' which he and Flaubert had seen just before they left Paris.

Langlois's technique had been to paint scenes on a continuous canvas screen. In order for them to be viewable to the considerable audiences he had in mind, they had necessarily to be large, and he had found it desirable to mount the heavy screen on cable so that it could be pulled past the viewing point by mechanical means. He found that this added to the effect, since dispensing with visible human agency strengthened the illusion that one was watching the events themselves.

"And he is doing one on Karnak?"

"That is so."

I was interested. I won't say that the idea came to me then and there, but a germ was planted. Years afterwards, when touring in Egypt had become the fashion and our business was well established, it grew into something.

Flaubert, however, was dismissive.

"It is mere spectacle," he said.

"But movement and colour can stimulate the imagination," I said, "in ways that a picture by itself cannot. When Maxime shows people one of his photographs, they will say, 'Ah, yes, that is Karnak.' But it will not give them a living impression as Langlois's panorama will."

"At least it will be accurate," said Maxime, displeased.

"And what is this 'living'?" said Flaubert. "Is mechanical succession life?"

"It can give the illusion of life," I maintained.

171

"Pah!" said Maxime.

"If it does," said Flaubert, "it does so only in the way that a roundabout in a country fair does: the horses go round and sometimes they go up and down, but only the children are deceived."

"And yet if things go fast enough—"

"Movement is of the surface," said Flaubert. "To find out if Maxime is a person or merely an automaton I have to go beneath the surface. I have to look into his mind."

"And what do you find there?" asked Maxime.

"Salacious thoughts."

They both laughed but I could tell that this was important to Flaubert. Later, much later, I realised that this must have been because it connected up with the issues that, deep down, were preoccupying him throughout the whole of the voyage: doubts about his vocation, doubts about himself and his talent, doubts about, even if writing was his vocation and he had the talent, in which direction to go.

So was Maxime right when he complained of Flaubert's being content just to sit there passively, watching the panorama of Egypt unwind before him? I think he may not have been. I think that all the time Flaubert was sitting there apparently doing nothing he was nevertheless thinking hard, thinking about the things that were all important to him, and which he had to resolve, or at least get out of the way, before he could move forward.

And when, at Philae, he had gone away by himself

into the colonnades, it was not, as Maxime supposed, because of indolence or because his boredom had become particularly acute, but because he had felt, like Miss Nightingale, the need to take stock, to come to terms, if only for the moment, with all the different, often contradictory possibilities that were working inside him.

To the west of Philae was another island, smaller than Philae and divided from it only by a thin channel, so narrow that on the *dahabeeyah* we could hear every sound from the village opposite. It was built among the ruins of a temple and a propylon jutted up incongruously from among the huts. Every morning we could see the women pounding grain for the evening meal and washing clothes at the water's edge. They often had children with them and sometimes the children would swim across to us and beg. One of the crew had a sister on the island and, mindful of Miss Nightingale's desire to meet some ordinary Egyptian women, I persuaded him to take us across and introduce us to her.

Although she was only sixteen, she was already a widow, with a four-year-old child. She lived in a two-room hut with her parents-in-law. One room was for the family, the other for the domestic animals. The room in which the family lived was, however, presentably clean although completely bare of furnishings. There was a raised clay platform at one end of the hut on which they slept in the winter; in the summer they slept outside.

We were offered flat durra cakes and honey.

There was a little debate about this between the woman and her brother. He felt, apparently, that we should have been offered bread, since cakes were only for women. His sister, who was plainly not greatly in awe of her brother, retorted that Miss Nightingale *was* a woman.

I intervened at this point and said I was sure that Miss Nightingale would be glad to try the cakes, as she was eager to see how women lived in Egypt. Our crewman, however, remained unhappy.

"The problem is, Miss Nightingale," I explained, "that our friend here feels that your grandeur entitles you to the status of male; whereas his sister clings to the view that you deserve only the privileges ordinary to womanhood."

Miss Nightingale considered gravely.

"While I would normally claim only those privileges due to my sex," she said, "I feel that to do so in this case would be to aggravate discord in a family which has received us very kindly. Would it answer, do you think, if I were to take a tiny piece of both?"

All this time a little girl had been hovering round us. She followed us, round-eyed, as we walked through the village and the next day we found her waiting for us when we disembarked from the *dahabeeyah*. She had swum across the channel that divided the islands. The ladies were alarmed on her behalf, but we were assured that such prowess was normal among the children of the island. For the rest of our stay at Philae she was inseparable from us. The ladies made something of a pet of her, and when we left, Miss Nightingale proposed, more than half seriously, to take her with us.

"My dear—" began Mr Bracebridge.

"We could find a kind home for her in Cairo," Miss Nightingale insisted, "where she could be brought up in the Christian faith and educated. Then she could go back and educate the other women of the island."

"But—"

"Have you not seen," said Miss Nightingale, "that the women there never pray? It is one of the things that is denied them, along with food equal to that given to men. And while that continues so, they cannot be lifted."

"Miss Nightingale," I said, "you must do no such thing. To take the child away from her mother, her family, would be monstrous! No matter how good your intentions."

"The mother—" began Miss Nightingale.

"Would no doubt agree," I cut in, "thinking that it would be in the child's best interests. But it would not be. It would be a monstrous, awful thing to do!"

Miss Nightingale was taken aback by my vehemence. I was, too, and feared I had gone too far. However, we heard no more of the proposal.

There were moments like that when she seemed particularly far away. But then there were also moments when she seemed to wish to come nearer. What form did she wish our relationship to take? At the end of our time on the island I was no more certain about how I was going to conduct myself towards her than I had been at the beginning.

Flaubert once bought a woman's hair. It was at Dakkeh, not far from Philae. He had admired her hair ornaments and, on a whim, asked how much it would cost to buy both hair and ornaments. Ten piastres, the woman's husband had replied immediately, and the deal was struck. The husband had done the shearing himself, while the woman wept bitterly.

"*Please*, Miss Nightingale! Yes, all movables. They are movables, are they not? Seasick? I'm afraid I couldn't say. Do chameleons get seasick? It is not a question I have hitherto encountered. No, it is more a question of them being dislodged during passage. Thrown off the wall. Would it break their backs? I don't know. I expect so. Yes, I agree that they have flexible spines, but—"

We were making ready to descend the Cataract. The crew had been up since before dawn, moving everything aft. Kitchen, *goullel*, boxes, hen-coop, all were brought back and made fast in front of the cabin door. Everything moveable was stowed below. In the cabins all small objects were being put away in boxes and lockers and anything loose was being tied down. Bed linen was being cleared away.

"There may be water, you see."

"In the cabins?"

"I'm afraid so. Waterproofs? Well, yes, if you have them. And boots. Umbrellas? It is not from the sky, Mrs Bracebridge, that the water is likely to come."

It would break over the front of the boat sweeping everything before it. That did not matter. The important thing was that it should not get inside, at least, not in such quantities as to make the *dahabeeyah* unstable. That was why now, at the last moment, the crew were going round making fast the hatches.

Exactly at dawn the two Cataract Sheikhs came on board with some forty or fifty of their men. They were not swimmers this time but oarsmen and as soon as they arrived they ran the oars out and settled down in their places, two men to an oar. The *dahabeeyah* moved out from the bank and at once began to make for the other, the Libyan side. We would not be going back by the way we had come up, through the broken rocks and waterfalls, but by a separate channel, the Big Bab.

I stationed the party on top of the boxes and hen-coop, as before, with their backs firmly against the front of the cabin but this time secured them with ropes. If the *dahabeeyah* met with a mishap during the descent, which was, unfortunately, not uncommon – although I did not tell them that – this would present problems, but that was the safest part of the boat and the more likely danger was of them being swept away.

177

"If you feel the water plucking at you, do not be alarmed. The ropes will keep you secure. You should be high enough to escape most of the water. And the apron that the crew is creating in front of you will help."

"We can always change afterwards," said Mr Bracebridge bravely.

The river seemed to be running faster than usual. Flecks of white water began to appear in front and at our sides. Ahead there was a continuous roar.

We suddenly saw that the two sheikhs had taken up their places, one forward at the prow, the other amidships where he could keep an eye on the oarsmen. The tiller was manned not by one man but by six, three on each side, big men, their chests bare.

The cliffs had closed in and we were running through a narrow strait. At the far end the water was tumultuous, white foam spitting up at the rocks, little eddies spinning round and whipping back. The roar became deafening.

Suddenly, the water in front of us seemed to tilt and a moment later the *dahabeeyah* too, seemed to tilt. Then we were at the lip of a monstrous rapid and tipping over, and the next instant we were plunging down, at a terrifying speed, the water crashing over our bows. On either side, rocks loomed up frighteningly close; loomed up and then fell away almost as we saw them.

The walls of rock closed in still more. We could almost touch them. There was no room to row, no time, either, with the boat moving at such speed. The men had shipped their oars but were standing by them, their eyes fixed intently on the second sheikh, who stood amidships, right in front of us, gently stroking his beard.

The *dahabeeyah* began to lurch heavily, hitting the water in front of it in a series of heavy jolts. Water crashed over the prow and then ran back, covering the entire deck and stopping at the boxes beneath us. Spray reached up over the top of the cabin. The water in front of us was seething and boiling.

And still the cliffs closed in. We felt, rather than heard, the *dahabeeyah* scrape the rock on either side. Suddenly there was a horrible grinding beneath and then that too fell away.

The boat seemed to quicken, there was another lip, on which the *dahabeeyah* hung poised, for, it seemed, eternity. Another tilt, which brought the rear of the boat right up until it seemed we were looking vertically downwards into the heart of the river itself, a seething, boiling cauldron, and then a mighty jolt which sent a huge wave straight up the deck at us. The next moment water was all about us and someone cried out, but the ropes held firm.

The great wave fell away and the boat levelled out. The deck was covered with water which slopped around and wouldn't go away. The boat seemed increasingly heavy to handle and yet we were still speeding madly onwards.

Then came more cries of alarm, this time from all the

party. We appeared to be heading straight at a massive wall of rock!

The sheikh raised his hand and the oarsmen made ready their oars but did not yet run them out. At the prow the other sheikh bent forward and the men at the tiller braced themselves. Then he, too, raised his hand, the men threw their whole, combined weight at the bar and, the next moment, the *dahabeeyah* swung round and we saw that the rapid made a sharp right turn. Almost before we had registered this, at the very same moment we made the turn, the men thrust their oars out and began rowing. The cliffs fell away, the river widened out and suddenly we were beyond the rocks and into calmer water. The roar was now behind us. We were through the Cataract.

Eleven

"No, no, they come back. To resume their bodies. In fact, some of them should be coming back just about now. The three thousand years of probation will have elapsed."

"You mean, we might meet them?"

"Certainly."

Mrs Bracebridge paused doubtfully. If it was hot among the bare rocks outside, it was even hotter in the tunnel that led to the tomb and the sweat was streaming down her face.

"I don't think I should care for that," she said.

"It depends in what form they come back. If they have loved the good you should be all right. If not, they may be like the gentleman we saw in the first tomb."

Mrs Bracebridge pushed the damp hair back off her face. It had been a long, exhausting morning.

"What was that like, dear? I'm afraid I don't recall."

"He came back in the form of a pig. That was because he had led such a horrid, sensual life while on earth."

"I think I may have missed that one."

"It was in the chamber. At one end of the wall you see him going up to Osiris for judgement, and then at the other you see him departing as a pig."

"The justice seems a little rough," said Mr Bracebridge.

"Oh, I don't know," said Miss Nightingale airily.

We had ridden up into the Valley of Kings that morning, leaving while it was still dark so that we could cover as much of the journey as possible in the cool of the day. A precaution we appreciated when the sun came up and we found ourselves in a long, rocky valley where the heat was soon shimmering along the tops of the cliffs, sending little heat eddies spiralling up and down the rocky faces. The path led slowly upwards until we came to a place where the donkeys branched off and headed for what was obviously an artificial passage that had been cut between the cliffs. Passing through this, we found ourselves in another valley, even more bleak and inhospitable than the first. There was not a blade of grass, hardly even a shadow, nothing to relieve the bare rock, except that in the cliff face there were occasional holes, which marked the ends of the tunnels that led down into the pharaohs' tombs. For here the pharaohs were buried not in pyramids but in chambers cut deep into the cliffs, as secluded and inaccessible as even Miss Nightingale would have wished.

Except that they had not proved inaccessible. The concealed entrances had been exposed centuries ago and the tombs had been reached by many, both those in search of treasure and those, like ourselves, who were merely curious. Today their chief protection was the heat. The cliffs trapped the sun and in the valley it was like a furnace. To do the walking and climbing necessary to enter the tombs was, in these conditions, enervating in the extreme. Even hardy travellers like the Bracebridges had found it tough going.

Miss Nightingale, however, seemed unaffected by such considerations. All morning she had scrambled ahead of us over the rocks, been the first to stoop into the tunnels and then the last to embark on the exhausting climb back to the surface.

"Of course," she said now, preoccupied, "if they were ordinary people and not pharaohs it would be different. The three thousand years is a privilege granted only to the elite. Ordinary people have to serve ten thousand years. But they do have this advantage, that at the end of every thousand years they are allowed to choose what life they will lead next. If they choose a virtuous life three times in succession they 'recover the use of their wings'. Or so, I believe, Plato says."

Mr Bracebridge signalled for the luncheon basket.

"If the reward of virtue," he said, "is to come back to a place like this, I think I might prefer to forgo it."

"Yes," said Miss Nightingale, "I am inclined to agree with you. Although, presumably once you had got back, you wouldn't have to stay here. You could go down into the cities."

Michael Pearce

The men carried the basket into the shady entrance to the tunnel and set about making ready a picnic luncheon. Miss Nightingale sat down on a rock.

"I think that is what I would do. I think if I were a pharaoh I would choose to come back in human form. And it would, of course, have to be a human of today. So . . ." She considered. "I think, I would come back as an Arab. And then I would go down into Luxor and see what I could do to help all those poor people there. Yes, that is what I would do. And," she said briskly, "this afternoon, when we go to our next tomb, I shall look out for Rameses and tell him so."

Every evening she made a list of the places she wanted us to visit the following day and noted the features that particularly interested her.

VALLEY OF KINGS
TOMB OF RAMESES THE FOURTH
   Ceiling (female figure encircling firmament, man
               supporting!)
TOMB OF RAMESES THE FIFTH
   Ceiling (astronomical)
   Hours (star on head. King: hourly review of his
             life – importance of reflection?)
TOMB OF SETI THE FIRST (Belzoni tomb)
   Underworld
   Walls   covered with texts

The Dragoman's Story

corridor 'Praisings of Ra'
Chamber 'Book of the Underworld'

She would give me the list and I would make all the
necessary arrangements before I went to bed. In the
morning we would set out early and cross the river by
small boat to where the asses would be waiting on the
other side. Their drivers would lead them into the river
so that we could mount them from the boat and not get
our feet wet wading ashore. Then we would ride inland on
whatever course Miss Nightingale had prescribed for us.

COLOSSI OF MEMNON (music)
SHEIKH ABD-EL-KOORNEH (private tombs)
DAYR EL BAHREE (temple)

The colossi rise straight up out of cultivated fields
which at the time of the inundation are covered with
water so that it seems as if the giant statues are standing
in a lake. There are two of them, both originally about
seventy feet high, and now somewhat damaged. The
northernmost one is held to emit a mysterious sound every
morning at sunrise, which Mr Bracebridge attributed to the
differential effect of heat and cold, the stone expanding
under the heat of the sun after contracting during the cold
of the night. Miss Nightingale asked if that was so, why
did not the other colossus made a noise too? And Mrs

185

Bracebridge, after consulting her guide book, pointed out that some people held that since the restoration of the statue by Septimus Severus *neither* of the colossi had produced any music.

Be that as it may, as we were leaving, a distinct note, as from the plucking of a harp, appeared to come from the colossus. We stopped for a moment, disconcerted, but then the mystery was explained by the sight of an Arab high up in its lap brandishing a musical instrument.

"It is a *joke*, Miss Nightingale."

"A characteristically demeaning one," she said haughtily. She was not much taken by the colossi. They lacked, she complained, the nobility of the figures of Abu Simbel.

Nor was she impressed by the tombs at Sheikh Abd-el-Koorneh. Of course, in those days the tombs had not been opened up to the extent that they have now, but it was possible to go inside some of them. The pictures on the walls were for the most part unexciting, consisting chiefly of processions, but there were many scenes of ordinary life, of people fishing and fowling and feasting, making music and working in the fields.

Miss Nightingale stole a glance at me.

"I am sure you will like these, Thomas."

I had to admit that I did in fact prefer these tombs to the ones in the Valley of the Kings, where the images were almost all of fearsome monsters and dark journeys through the underworld. The tombs at Abd-el-Koorneh were not for kings but for their officers and it seemed

186

to me that they had a much more cheerful time of it than did their masters. It was like, I ventured, the rule of the Roundheads, with the Puritans leading a gloomy life on top and everyone else having a splendid time down below.

Miss Nightingale was displeased.

"I," she said primly, "am inclined to side with Lepsius when he says that the Egyptians tend to reduce their graves to a book of trades."

THE RAMESSEUM
the four sacred boats (shrines – compare Moses's imitation of them in the Ark and the Tabernacle)
The sacred library (books of Hermes)
Colossus of Rameses II (largest in Egypt).

"No, Thomas, they were not all named Rameses. Some were called Sethos and some Thothmosis. Although, admittedly, there were a lot of Rameseses in the Twentieth Dynasty. However, my favourite is Rameses the Second, and he belongs to the Nineteenth Dynasty. Do you know why he is my favourite, Thomas? It is because although he was a great warrior and won a lot of battles, he also led a life of service. That was what all pharaohs were supposed to do. They had to serve God and they had to serve their people. But there was no contradiction between the two. All they had to do was follow the laws that God had laid down, because the law in Egypt was aimed at the people's

good, or so Diodorus says. What the pharaoh had to do
was give the law energy, and that was what Rameses, my
Rameses, was so good at.

"But he did much more than that. He built temples and
maintained the waterworks and created cities, oh, and
lots of other things besides. It was all offered as service,
Thomas, because that was what he wanted, he wanted to
serve both God and his people, both together, and that
was why he was so wise, Thomas, and so great.

"But what *would* he think, Thomas, if he came back
today? His three thousand years is about up, and what
would he find?"

KARNAK
   the great hall
   the approach (dromos of sphinxes, *four pairs* of
     propyla)
   scale!!

"*Rubbish*, Thomas, that's what he would find. It almost
fills the great hall. And it's growing all the time. All those
wonderful things – *disappearing*! That lovely Sethos over
there, the rubbish reaches right up to the chin already and
soon it will cover it entirely. It will go and no one will
even know that it ever existed!

"And what would it take to put it right, at least here at
Karnak, to clear all the rubbish away? A hundred pounds,
that's all. The sort of money that Abbas Pasha spends in
bribes every week or on his own sensual pleasures. But

it's not just that, is it? Not just money. It's will and energy,
yes, and service, too. Oh, for a Rameses in Egypt today
and not an Abbas Pasha!"

MEDINA TABOU
    Pavilion (note battlements, unusual in Egypt)
    the great courtyards (reliefs esp.)
    the portrait heads (Etruscan, Sicilian, Libyan etc.)

"Ugh! This is where it all begins to go wrong, Thomas.
The barbarity! More like the castle of some savage chief
than a civilised Egyptian temple! And then the reliefs:
very fine, no doubt, but the cruelty – the prisoners tied
under the axle, the chiefs bringing him *hands*! Of course,
it's Rameses the Third, Thomas, not Rameses the Second.

"The coronation scenes – vulgar throughout. Just like
Napoleon crowning his wife! And then what happens to
the wife? Look, here she is, pushed aside, up on a sort
of shelf. But that's not the worst of it, look at this: the
harem scenes!"

In one, the king sits at ease in his chair while a young
girl, wearing earrings and necklace but not much else,
holds a lotus blossom to his nose.

"He is chucking her under the chin, Thomas! That is
what I mean by vulgar."

In another, they are playing draughts.

"Charming? No, Thomas, that is not what I call charming! Companionship? Well, yes, of a sort. Of a sort,

Thomas! But is it the companionship of a Rameses the Second and a Nefertari? Where is the respect, the honour, the love? No, Thomas, this is decline. This is where it begins to go wrong. Oh, I know you can't just draw a straight line from then to today, but have we ever recovered the beauty of the relationship between Rameses and Nefertari? Not in Egypt, at any rate. Look around you, Thomas. A female elephant has a greater sense of worth than a woman in Egypt today."

Lists. Flaubert, of course, made them too, only in his case the lists were the ingredients of meals, the ornaments of camels, the perfumes and oils in a scent-seller's shop. I had seen that as related to his thirst for information, the kind of curiosity that had made him, from my point of view, a model tourist. But now I see that it could have been related to his work as a novelist. At the time I had thought it perhaps a way of shutting out the vocational doubts he appeared to have and that may, indeed, have been so, although not in quite the way that I had thought. The gathering of material for a book as yet unformulated in his mind but which might at some time get written was, possibly, a way of reassuring himself that he was still in some sense a writer. And perhaps the degree of his need for reassurance was sometimes reflected in what had struck me then as a kind of compulsiveness in the list making.

But was there not something equally compulsive about

the passion for lists that overtook Miss Nightingale at Thebes? Initially I attributed it to the habit of over-earnest planning ahead that I had noticed in the hotel in Cairo when I had come upon her copying out plans of temples. 'I do like to see things clearly in my mind beforehand,' she had said then and I had taken it as evidence of a tendency towards abstraction which, indeed, subsequent experience had confirmed. But now, as the lists multiplied and seemed to take over the charting of our lives, we all, I think, began to feel that there was something excessive in her zeal for them. They drove us on at such a pace as to leave little room for our lives to take on a shape of their own.

The Bracebridges, indeed, dropped out after a while, pleading exhaustion. Miss Nightingale did not mind. She had me.

But in what capacity? Guide? No longer. Miss Nightingale had taken over the direction of the tour into her own hands. Companion? Certainly. But more than companion. Confidant, then? Yes, if to be the recipient of an almost continuous commentary on everything we saw was to enter into her confidence. Yet she never spoke, not while we were at Thebes, at any rate, of that inner wrestle that had preoccupied her, on and off, for almost the whole of our journey. It was as if she had, for the moment, set it aside. Pupil, perhaps, then? There was more than a little of that in our relationship, yes. Certainly she seemed to have a relish for instruction. More, she had a particular relish – or did I fancy that? – for instructing me. Now I know this may have been just because I was more amenable to instruction than the Bracebridges would have been, but I do not believe that was all there was to it. I sensed that she found a particular pleasure, a particular excitement, you might almost say, in instructing me.

Lover, then? No.

There was no hint of that. She kept her distance and I kept mine. She had reset the distance on the morning after the incident on the top deck and I had no choice other than to accept it. The distance stemmed as much from social as from personal reasons. She owed a duty to her parents, or felt she did, as Mr Bracebridge had made clear, and one could not but respect that.

As I say, there was never any hint. Except, perhaps, that particular relish. Or do I fancy that?

KOORNEH (temple, not tombs)
  son/father, father/son

"You see, Thomas, it was built by Sethos the First in memory of his father, Rameses the First; but then finished by *his* son, Rameses, the Second, my Rameses, in honour of him. It is a beautiful expression of the love and duty owed by one generation to another."

  the great hall

"The thing about the hall, Thomas, is that it was also

where the assembly used to meet, with the king presiding. In that way religion and governance could come together. I think that expresses a great truth, Thomas. You see, an individual, even a great individual like Rameses, cannot lift a society by himself. There has to be something wider, and that can only be religion. But that is what went wrong. Oh, I know that Christianity itself is not without fault here, but while Egypt was Christian, there was still hope, at least in one respect, and that was a very important respect. Women still had a chance. But what has replaced it!

"I know one must always respect religion, any religion, and I do. But, you see, Thomas, if women don't matter, *nothing* matters. And that is what has gone wrong in Egypt."

DAYR-EL-MEDEENEH (only Ptolemaic not classical)
   but see sanctuary

In the sanctuary the king is offering sacrifice to two figures of Hathor simultaneously. In one case she is the usual animal with the head of a cow. In the other she is a woman.

"If this means on the one hand our animal nature and on the other our intellectual nature, and that they have to be kept in balance, then that is a very sophisticated idea and one that we in Europe often get wrong, tending to elevate the one at the expense of the other. What do you think, Thomas? That this side of the temple is all about women and the other side all about men, and so that what this means is that woman must recognise the animal part of her nature? Well, no, Thomas, I don't think so."

We were at Thebes for three weeks, which enabled our mail to catch up with us. In one of the first sacks we opened was a letter to me from Aimée.

The other morning a little mite came to see us. Her name is Caroline and she is nine months old, which makes her about the same age as our little Louis. They are both at the crawling stage, except that she is much speedier than he is, nipping about and leaving him – well, not exactly standing, that is an accomplishment daily promised but as yet deferred – but sitting, rather. We put the two of them together to see how they would get on. Of course, they didn't really play together but played happily side by side. Except that Caroline seized one of Louis's toys and sped off with it. Louis sat there astonished for a moment but then made after her. It took him some time, I must admit, to catch up with her but when he did, he grabbed back the toy and then, in very ungentlemanly fashion, gave her a cuff. Men are, alas, men in our family.

Which reminds me of your Miss Nightingale and the woman question. I do admire her position. It makes me think about my own. Do I assert my

own value enough? Too much, my mother says;
my father says I hold my own. Well, perhaps that
is enough for my own case. But what of the more
general case, complicated as it is by my living in
a Muslim country? I tell Miss Nightingale that no
one knows what goes on behind the closed doors
of a Muslim household and that there is a lot more
give and take than she might think. But that is the
private sphere, she says, what about their position
in the public sphere? ah, well . . .

But, truly, is it so very different in France? I asked
Monsieur Flaubert and he said that the Arabs use
the same word, *almeh*, for 'learned woman' as they
do for 'prostitute' and that this expresses a truth
which applies even more in France. But then, says
Maxime, the only women Flaubert appears able to
talk to are either prostitutes or intellectuals, so it is
hardly surprising if he confuses the two.

Going back to little Caroline and Louis: do the
differences that show themselves at such an early
age rule out the notion of absolute equality? I
have an uneasy suspicion that Caroline will always
run rings round Louis but does that mean they
can never be equal? Of course, 'equal' does not
have to mean the same as 'same' and one person of a pair can be superior in one respect and
the other in another. For my part, I have always
taken it for granted that women were put into

the world to guide men. I mean that, of course, in a general sense which should not be applied too particularly. In particular, it should not be applied to the case of you and Miss Nightingale. I fear, from what you say in your letter, that you may be yielding yourself to her guidance a little too readily.

And I feared that Aimée might be yielding herself a little too readily to the guidance of Maxime. It was Maxime now, I noticed, not Monsieur du Camp, whereas it was still Monsieur Flaubert. Well, that at least was something. If Aimée was bestowing her favours, at least she was not doing so broadcast.

I must say, I found the letter disquieting in other respects, too. Clearly she had been in further correspondence with Miss Nightingale or, if not, then Miss Nightingale's ideas had gone on working within her. I had hoped that when I took Miss Nightingale off up the river, that would be an end of the matter. Evidently it was not.

Then another thought struck me. *When* had she asked Flaubert and *when* had Maxime made his silly comment? Before they left? Or was she in intimate correspondence with them, too? I looked at the date on the letter. It told me nothing. It was about the time they had intended to leave Cairo so the letter could have been written before their departure. What was clear, however, was that Aimée's relationships with them had progressed.

And what of her charge about my own relationship with Miss Nightingale?

beetles
gods
archers
those little blue saucers
soul houses (small)

"They are for presents, Thomas, little mementoes of our journey that I can give to aunts, uncles, nephews."

The beetles were the scarabs of ancient Egypt, small, faithful imitations sometimes cut from semi-precious stones like cornelian or amethyst, more often of glazed earthenware. The gods were clay, too, often only an inch or so long, little figures with animal heads, of ape or ibis or hippopotamus. The archers were little wooden models often buried with the dead, the saucers were the earthenware ones buried in the tombs, the soul houses sometimes wood, more often clay.

"They are unlikely, of course, to be genuine."

"I would prefer them to be genuine."

"In that case they will probably have been stolen."

"Hum. Are there no other possibilities?"

"One can sometimes come upon – but it would take a bit of looking."

Michael Pearce

"Thomas, *do* you think? Would you mind?"

soap
fly-whisks (ours are quite worn out!)
candles (I know, but we get through them at such an
awful rate!)
goggles (I've lost mine)

"You don't mind, do you? Say if you do."
But somehow it wasn't easy to.

198

Twelve

Ever since we had started on our return journey we had been aware that the water level in the river was falling. Now, as we set out from Luxor after spending more than three weeks ashore, the fall was marked. The banks had retreated on both sides leaving a broad expense of hard baked mud at their foot. Here and there the mud was green with newly planted watermelons. Each separate plant had a little house thatched with palm leaves built over it. The lupins and lentils which on our journey upstream had lined the water's edge were now high up on the banks. Behind them the fields which had then been green had now turned with incredible suddenness to gold. New sandbanks, some of them hundreds of yards in length, had appeared in the river and the *reis* stationed himself permanently in the bows peering at the channels ahead.

It had become very hot. In an effort to keep the *dahabeeyah* habitable, the crew hung wet sails over the sides and suspended towels from the ceilings of the cabins, which they dampened every half hour. Along the banks, the buffaloes standing in the shallows waded in deeper until the water was up over their shoulders.

The river shimmered in the heat. After an hour or so, even if you were wearing eyeshades or goggles, the glitter of the water became overwhelming. The Bracebridges took to spending more and more of the day below in the more restful darkness of their cabin. Miss Nightingale and I, however, remained on deck. It was as if, now that the end of our voyage was approaching, she was hungry not to miss anything. She seemed, nevertheless, more calm, more at ease with herself. The urgency that had possessed her throughout our stay in Thebes seemed to have abated.

One afternoon we were sitting up there by ourselves, she with a book in her hand, which, however, she had not opened since lunch, I idly scanning the banks. We had not spoken for some time. She seemed to have fallen into a private reverie.

Suddenly she said, "He spoke to me, you know."

"Spoke?"

"God. He spoke to me."

"Indeed?" I said cautiously.

"Yes. It was at Koorneh. That little temple there. You remember I went and sat by myself in the colonnade. We had been rushing about so much, the whole time we were at Thebes, and I wanted, well, I just wanted to be quiet, I suppose, so I went and sat in the shade.

And it was so lovely there that I sat there for ages.
The sun moved round and I had to keep moving, too,
to stay in the shadow. And all the time I was looking
at that wonderful view, the fields, the river stretching
away – you could trace it by the line of palm trees –
and then through the palms a glimpse of the temple at
Luxor, which looks much better when you see it from far
away; you don't see the human excrescences. And then
there are all the palm trees, you don't realise there are so
many when you're just riding along, but when you look
from a distance, you're surprised, it's all green. And in
one of the groves a woman was walking with a pot upon
her head, and it was so beautiful, just like a scene from
the Bible. So peaceful! And, well, I suppose it was His
peace that was entering into me. And then He spoke."

I could not think what to say. Eventually, I managed
something like, "Yes. Well. I see." And then, as that did
not seem enough, "And – and what did He say?"

"He called me to His service."

Flaubert, the whole time I knew him, never mentioned
the word 'service' except, possibly, in connection with
his official mission, when, if he did use it, it was entirely
ironically. Yet in a way this was odd, for the example
that Miss Nightingale gave me when I asked her what
she meant by service was that of a doctor. Flaubert's own
father was a doctor and you might, perhaps, have expected
this to influence him. The person she actually mentioned

was old Bosquet and this, too, was a surprise to me, for somehow I had never thought of Aimée's father in quite that way before. He had always seemed to me particularly matter of fact about his work. Perhaps all doctors are like that and perhaps Flaubert's father was like that, so that Flaubert had grown up thinking of his father's work as something akin to that of a shoe maker. Or perhaps his father had taken a view of his profession that was more in accord with Miss Nightingale's and his son had reacted against it.

However that be, service, in Miss Nightingale's sense, did not seem to be a factor in whatever Flaubert intended to do in life. Nor, I must confess, had it hitherto been in mine.

"But, surely, Thomas, you will admit that there is more to life – more to work – than merely pecuniary gain?"

Well, yes, indeed. That was what had brought me out to Egypt in the first place. That was what had nourished my ambition to be an artist. That—

"An artist, Thomas! Surely not. For that you need—"

Talent. And luck. And self-belief. And commitment. The sort of commitment that I now see Flaubert showed and which I suspect precluded him from paying much attention to the kind of service that Miss Nightingale was interested in.

During the voyage I had become sadly aware that the talent I possessed was calculated more to please the nursery than the connoisseur. Beside even Mrs Bracebridge's work

I could see that my own lacked technique and, more than technique, the kind of conviction that the work of a genuine artist, such as my friend, Jack, possesses. Beside Jack I was nothing – and even he was finding it hard to make a living.

"—private means," finished Miss Nightingale, shaking her head kindly but firmly.

She was right, and not just for that reason. There was no prospect of my becoming an artist. It was merely one of those foolish dreams that one has in youth, when all the world seems open and everything seems possible. Nor was the prospect of my earning a living as a photographer any more realistic. It would be today and, indeed, I have sometimes thought of establishing a photographic business as a private sideline. But what you have to remember is that at that time the tour was in its infancy and the number of visitors coming to the country still relatively small. Even I knew that if I was to make my way as a photographic artist, it could be only in another country. What I had hazily in mind was setting myself up in some European capital city such as Paris or Vienna and gaining a name initially as a purveyor of images of the Orient. You see that even in my dreams I was still holding fast to that vision I had of myself as an interpreter of Egypt, an intermediary between Europeans and the Orient.

Well, of course, it came to nothing. Or, perhaps, not quite to nothing, for today I make considerable use of photographs and other illustrative material in the brochures we send out to clients. I sometimes think that the ambitions and ideas we formulate for ourselves when we are young are ones we remain true to, only they come to be expressed in a way quite different from that we had originally intended.

Be that as it may, all I knew at the time was that the prospect of my becoming a professional photographer was as unlikely as that of my becoming any other kind of artist.

Yet in those foolish dreams of mine there was something not entirely out of accord with Miss Nightingale's point of view. I did think there was more to life, and more to work, than pecuniary gain. In my way I rejected an ordinary working life, the life of a clerk, say, as firmly as Flaubert rejected the various career possibilities put forward to him by his mother. Like him, I looked for something larger. Where, perhaps, I had gone wrong was in allowing myself to be too attracted by his and Maxime's talk of the claims of art. Were not the claims of mankind equally strong? So, at least, I began to be persuaded by Miss Nightingale.

"You see, Thomas, you were right. Do you remember that day, back in Cairo, when we rode down to the river to see the *dahabeeyah*? And on the way we saw those poor creatures crawling out of their huts? I could hardly believe that they were human beings, they were so reduced. I thought that their wretchedness must mean that they were not really God's work, that He had somehow rejected them. And you rebuked me, Thomas, quite properly, and said that God does not reject people. Well, you didn't actually put it quite like that. What you said – and I shall never forget this – was that their condition was not theological, it was something man-made, and that if it was man-made then it could be put right. I shall always be grateful to you for saying that, because, Thomas, at that moment I was in danger, great spiritual danger. It is only when I am in my dark moods that I think like that, and what I have come to see, Thomas, is that it is those dark moments, those doubts, that are the work of the Devil, and not – not those poor people.

"But you were wrong, Thomas, at least, not completely right, in one respect. You said that man could put things right. But I don't think he can, not by himself, in a world ruled by Abbases. The task is too great. It is something that only God can do. But for that He needs our help.

"And I think that is what God has been trying to tell me. You see, I thought that what He wanted was for me to devote myself to Him in church and private prayer, but I don't think He wants that at all, at least, not just that. He wants me to go out and work for Him, to go out into the world among ordinary people and do His service there."

Service: that was the thought towards which all her inner debate had been leading and which she believed God to have finally crystallised for her. It was what she took from her contemplation of the pharaohs and in particular from the life of Rameses the Second, and perhaps it was reinforced by her perception of the needs of the Egyptian poor. The election she had made in the Valley of Kings on behalf of any returning pharaoh was the one that she had finally chosen for herself.

And it was one towards which, little by little, I found her drawing me.

In Wiltshire, where I come from, we didn't really think much about the service of mankind. It was all we could do, as it was, to keep going ourselves. The service of mankind was something we left to those who could afford it. Now, however, as the hot days slipped by, I began to think about it quite a lot. I had always prided myself on possessing a countryman's hard-headedness on such matters. Now I began to see that hard-headedness by itself might not be such a good thing. There had always been, as I have mentioned before, another side to me. Now, as Miss Nightingale talked on about her ambitions and aspirations, that other side came to seem more and more important. I have always been, as Aimée says, a creature of enthusiasms and now a new enthusiasm was developing within me. The prospect of devoting myself to some great cause was coming to seem increasingly attractive. What that cause was I was not sure but I was confident in Miss Nightingale's, or God's, ability to define it. Miss Nightingale herself, convinced now that God's purpose for her would soon be revealed, seemed

more and more to take it for granted that I would be an
adjunct in her pursuit of that purpose. If God had called
Miss Nightingale to His service, she, as heat-dazed day
succeeded to heat-dazed day, was calling me to hers.

Something of my new preoccupation must have entered
into my letters to Aimée for in one of the last replies
I received from her, just before we reached Cairo, she
said:

> What is all this about service? It sounds most
> unlike you, dear. Are you sure you have not caught
> something from Miss Nightingale's chameleons?

Our last port of call before we reached Cairo was
Memphis: city of columned courtyards and sacred groves,
of obelisks and pylons and avenues of sphinxes, of the
famous artificial lake over which the dead were ferried,
and of the great Temple of Phthah.

"Where once Moses walked, Thomas. According to
Strabo (or is it Manetho?) he was a priest at Heliopolis.
Strabo says that he wanted to rid Egypt of what he called
the worship of animals – those animal-headed gods, of
course – and substitute the idea of an invisible, unitary
deity. That was a great thought, Thomas, a giant leap
in man's mental horizon, and it is not surprising that it
should arise here, where there was such a tradition of
spiritual thinking. But why couldn't the Egyptians accept

it? I think it was because it was too great, too daring for them, and so he took it to the Hebrews. And that in itself was very daring, quite extraordinary when you come to think of it, for as a priest he was a member of Egypt's elite and the Hebrews were just slaves. To him they would have seemed like savages."

Moses had been very much in her thoughts as we approached Memphis.

"I've always admired him, Thomas. He was obviously such a very able and cultivated man. And then to step down from all that privilege and go among the humblest of people . . ."

She was eager now to see the precincts which once had known him, as if by standing there she could capture something of his presence.

We came first to the famous Palm Forest; not really a forest by European standards but certainly a larger grove than any we had seen before in Egypt. Beneath the trees, unusually, there was grass, not sand, and in the grass hundreds of dwarf irises. We stopped for a moment, delighted, and Mrs Bracebridge wished to dismount and pick some for pressing and putting in her album. Miss Nightingale, however, impatient of temporal beauties, was all for hurrying on.

But where *was* Memphis? We came out from the palm trees and all we could see were some huge mounds about thirty or forty feet high, with here and there some crumbling brickwork showing through the sand.

The Dragoman's Story

"Is this all?" said Miss Nightingale.

The guide books should have prepared her but this time she had een unwilling to accept their authority. She could not believe that anything as great as Memphis, the ancient capital of Egypt, for a time the largest city in the world, should have disappeared so totally. In her mind's eye she had seen it so clearly, with its towering buildings and shady walks, its mighty colossi and the sculpture that was the wonder of the ancient world. She had peopled it with priests and philosophers talking earnestly in the colonnades, had strained to overhear them, had almost thought she might, for a moment, beneath the huge columns, converse with the ghost of Moses.

Disappointed, she wandered for a while among the mounds, hoping for at least a glimpse of some broken statuary, a round of column, or part of the carved lintel of a door, but all she found were a few pot sherds and occasional patches of powdering brickwork exposed by the goats as they clambered up to tear at the sparse scrub on the top of the mound.

As we rode back through the palm trees, however, we came upon a colossus lying in its face in mud from which the water of a nearby pond had newly retreated. It was the great statue of Rameses that had once stood before the Temple of Phthah and there seemed something sadly appropriate in finding it lying there like that.

Miss Nightingale dismounted from her donkey and

209

stood there quietly for a moment. Then she went up to it and ran her fingers over the huge stone face.

"It seems like sacrilege," she said, "but it's not meant like that. Treat it as affection, Rameses!"

She climbed back up on to her donkey.

"Goodbye, Rameses!" she called, as we turned away. "Goodbye, old, wonderful, dead Egypt!"

I had failed, of course. It was dead Egypt she was bidding reluctant farewell to, not live Egypt. When I pointed out to her that there was still Cairo to come, she looked at me in surprise.

"But Cairo isn't Egypt, is it?"

The Egypt that had captured her imagination was an Egypt that was past. I had wanted her to see the Egypt that was there. I had known that would be difficult for, in my experience, Europeans always bring to Egypt the prejudices and stalenesses of their own way of living. For her to truly see Egypt she would need to look with fresh eyes. I had thought, for some reason, that I might be able to bring this about. But now I saw that she had never really been interested in what was there, that what had drawn her was an abstraction. For my newer Egypt she had no time at all. It contained too many things she disliked: corruption, brutality, the disadvantagement of women. It contained other things, too, which I had wanted to show her, but those things she could not see.

Thirteen

"Again?"

"Yes, Miss Nightingale, I am afraid so."

"But they have been to say their farewells twice already!"

"This is not exactly to say farewell."

It was, in fact, an attempt to get money out of her for the third time that day. When the crew had first come to the hotel, early that morning, they had been so affected by the prospect of losing their kindly friends that they had burst into tears. This had so melted the ladies that they in turn had begun to weep, and soon tears were flowing as abundantly as the *bahksheesh* they provoked. So moved were the crew that they had returned for a second time later in the morning to protest once more their desolation, with the same result; except that afterwards I had suggested that enough was enough. Now, however, three of them had appeared with a particular problem affecting a member of the crew of whom she had seemed especially fond, which they wished to share with her.

211

Michael Pearce

"It appears, Miss Nightingale, that Abdul wants to get married but lacks the hundred and fifty piastres required to purchase the necessary *tob* for the lady in question."

"And he hopes I will supply it?"

"Knowing your generous heart, yes."

"Is he really going to get married?"

"Why not, given the money?"

"Hum. What do you advise?"

"Say that you will leave seventy-five piastres with the consul, to whom he may apply after a year if he has saved the further seventy-five piastres."

Abdul looked a little glum when this was put to him but, after consulting his companions, squared his shoulders resolutely.

"And tell him," said Miss Nightingale, "that he is not to beat her!"

"Oh, that won't be necessary," said Abdul confidently. "She's just a simple countrywoman and not one of these Cairenes."

My own marriage was not long delayed. Aimée, too, said that enough was enough and that, given my new prospects with Mr Shepheard, and the enormous amount of money I appeared to have made out of my two parties that spring, there was no reason why it shouldn't take place immediately. Whatever hopes Madame Bosquet had of an alliance with either Flaubert or Maxime were put firmly aside.

"They are not," said Aimée, "the marrying kind. Besides, when a woman is choosing a husband, as opposed to a lover, she has to bear in mind the figure he will cut as a father. Does he, for a start, like children? And then, what prospect is there of him being able to occupy them while she gets on with more important things? However great the talents of Messieurs Flaubert and du Camp in other directions, for parenthood, from my observation of them, they have no talent at all. Whereas you, my dear, with all your shortcomings – given a guiding hand, of course."

My interest in devoting myself to the service of mankind did not long survive my return to Cairo. Was it necessary, asked Aimée, to be quite so absolute? Were we not all, in our different ways, serving mankind through the work we contributed to society? To talk of doctors was all very well but in her experience they were just ordinary people who did their job and liked their aperitif as much as anyone else. Was not the man who brought them that aperitif performing a valuable service too? Old Bosquet himself would certainly have said so.

Ah, yes, I said, but we were talking about disinterested service. Were we, asked Aimée? Her father was an amiable fellow and wished his patients well, and that may, indeed, have had something to do with his choosing to become a doctor, but if any of them thought they were going to get treatment without paying for it, then they were badly mistaken. Disinterestedness, she said

213

pointedly, was for those, like Miss Nightingale, who did not have to support themselves and – even more pointedly and rather spitefully, I thought – were unlikely ever to be called upon to support a family. Relations between Aimée and Miss Nightingale seemed to have cooled markedly since our return.

Aimée did, though, follow her later career with considerable interest. There was still, of course, no hint of that career when Miss Nightingale left Egypt. She had made up her mind during her time on the Nile that she could best do God's will by devoting herself to some great end which would be for the benefit of mankind. As yet, however, she had not hit on the exact form that would take although there was, perhaps, something significant in a letter she wrote to me just before her boat sailed from Alexandria.

This is my last day in Egypt and I really think it is one of the most curious days I have ever spent. Yesterday I went to the hospital of the Sisters of St Vincent and this morning I went there again, really just to say goodbye, but there was a Mother Superior there newly arrived from Australia, who asked to be shown round, and I went with her. Yesterday, I had seen the schools, and they were impressive enough, but this morning we spent more time in the dispensary. It is all run by the sisters, of course, and so calmly, so efficiently – a cut above anything else

The Dragoman's Story

I have seen in Egypt in that respect, I may tell you!
– and in such a different spirit.

And then (it was an engagement I had asked for
and so couldn't get out of) we went to visit the
wife of Sayid Pasha. It was, of course, in the harem
apartments and to get to them we had to go through
gardens with fountains playing, marbled halls ditto
and luxurious room after luxurious room, until at
last we came upon her, sitting alone on a divan in a
vast hall. Apart from the divan, the room was empty.
There wasn't a thing there that she might occupy
herself with – no books, no musical instrument, not
even any embroidery. You gathered the impression
that she didn't do a thing for herself – wasn't allowed
to! Coffee was brought for us (and bubble pipes,
encrusted with diamonds, for us to smoke!) but a
slave did the pouring. The whole time she sat there
smiling gently and sweetly with her hands in her lap.
And that, one feels, is pretty much how she spent her
days. The boredom! I felt so sorry for her . . .

I asked if, perhaps, there were children, but she
said no. She had, however, an adopted daughter,
who was brought in, looking very sweet in a lovely
yellow satin dress with a train and a little turban.
Her mother was obviously very fond of her but even
here, you felt, slaves did everything for the child and
she herself was allowed to do little. She was cut off
from life at every turn. I couldn't have borne it.

And that seems the problem with a woman's life here. She is cut off from life. Oh, I know a pasha's wife is an extreme case and that in poorer families necessity would require her engagement with at least some household tasks. But her life would still have to be led largely within the house and she would be denied the larger life that exists outside. And then, of course, even within the house she might have to share her privacy with others, other wives, other women. The harem principle strikes at women in so many ways. I tell you, Thomas, that if there is hell on earth, I saw it this morning. And if there is heaven, perhaps I saw that this morning, too – the Sisters' Dispensary.

Maxime wrote to me, too, after he had left, from Constantinople, to tell me that both he and Flaubert had caught syphilis.

They had called in at Cairo on their way back, but that was two months after my own return, and they had stayed for only a few days. They had done their sightseeing there before they had set out up the Nile and this was only to hand back the *dahabeeyah* and complete necessary formalities. There was hardly time for Maxime to do as he had promised and introduce me to the arts and techniques of photography. In any case, my heart was no longer in it.

During the four or five days that they were in Cairo I

216

saw very little of Flaubert. He spent much of his time in his room writing letters. I asked Maxime if Flaubert had resolved his career doubts or, at least, the career doubts his mother had had on his behalf. Maxime said there appeared to have been little progress. It was then that he complained of Flaubert's indolence during the voyage, of his appearing to be content just to sit there passively and watch Egypt unfolding 'like a panorama' before him. Of course, Flaubert's great achievements, like Miss Nightingale's, still lay in the future at this point. *Madame Bovary* did not appear until 1856. He did begin writing it, however, in the year following his return from Egypt and I like to think that his apparent passivity concealed not just the inner wrestle he was having over his doubts about his future but also his early thinking about his great novel. Perhaps, if that is true, he took with him from Egypt more than I had supposed.

And perhaps it is true of other books too. Aimée has just been reading an article which points out that Gustave left an unfinished novel behind him when he died in which his two central characters, Bouvard and Pecuchet, were intended as the embodiment of bourgeois conventionality and stupidity. The name Bouvard, even after all these years, rang a bell. It was what Flaubert called me when I was telling him about my forthcoming marriage to Aimée.

"Congratulations, Bouvard," he said to me. "It is a suitably bourgeois thing for you to do."

217

"Bouvard?"

He smiled and shook me by the hand.

"Thom-ass, of course."

"They don't really change," said Miss Nightingale. "At least, if they do, it's all on the surface. When they're angry, they go bright yellow. When they're scared, they go brown, with purple spots. But underneath they're just the same."

She was talking about her chameleons, of course.